NOAH BOYD

AGENT X

HARPER

An Imprint of HarperCollinsPublishers

This book is a work of fiction. References to real people, events, establishments, organizations, or locales are intended only to provide a sense of authenticity, and are used fictitiously. All other characters, and all incidents and dialogue, are drawn from the author's imagination and are not to be construed as real.

HARPER

An Imprint of HarperCollins*Publishers*
10 East 53rd Street
New York, New York 10022-5299

Copyright © 2011 by Noah Boyd
ISBN 978-0-06-182703-7

First Harper premium printing: August 2011
First William Morrow paperback international printing: February 2011
First William Morrow special paperback printing: February 2011
First William Morrow hardcover printing: February 2011

Printed in the United States of America

Visit Harper paperbacks on the World Wide Web at
www.harpercollins.com

10 9 8 7 6 5 4 3 2 1

For my wife, Patti,
who has always grown stronger
the more impossible things become

AGENT X

BEFORE

KATE BANNON THOUGHT SHE WAS HAVING A NIGHTMARE, BUT actually she was dying.

Only her nagging self-awareness, even in this somnolent state, was forcing her to remember that she didn't have nightmares. The frightening images had always been there—people shooting at her, falling endlessly from towering buildings, running through thicker and thicker sand to escape something unknown—but her reaction to them had always been as an indifferent observer, curious and analytical. If the "danger" persisted, she would simply tell herself it was a dream and wake up. And that's what she had to do now, wake up and find out what was causing the chaotic images in her head.

She sat up and felt dizzy, the blood pounding in the top of her head. It hurt too much to be a dream. She felt nauseous and remembered driving home after the Thanksgiving Eve get-together at one of the local FBI watering holes with a large group of people from headquarters. She remembered having a glass of wine, and then a good-looking guy she didn't know brought her a small glass of—what did he say it was?—Drambuie. She had never tasted it before and took a mouthful. Finding it too bitter for her liking, she set it down and didn't touch it again. It must have been strong, because she soon started feeling woozy and decided to leave.

Throwing her legs over the side of the bed, she worked her feet into slippers and stood up. As soon as she was fully upright, she felt light-headed and had trouble balancing herself. With a hand on the wall, she started toward the kitchen. Walking left her short of breath. That couldn't be from alcohol. That's when she heard the low rumbling. She continued to the kitchen and saw that the door to the garage was open. Now she could clearly hear her car running.

Without warning, her knees started to buckle, and she realized that she was not suffering from what she had drunk but from carbon monoxide poisoning. Carefully, she stepped down the three stairs into the garage, which was filled with the haze of exhaust fumes. The car door was locked, and she could see the keys in the ignition.

The garage's outside door was only a few feet away, and she lurched to it. Taking hold of the knob, she tried to turn it, but her grip failed her. She pushed on the door clumsily with her body weight but couldn't rotate the knob far enough to open it. Even using both hands, she couldn't get it to release. Next to the door, in a holder fastened to the wall, was a remote-control unit for the overhead door. She pressed the button, but nothing happened.

Beginning to panic now, she pressed it repeatedly, but still the door didn't rise. She tried to remember the last time she had changed the battery, but her mind refused to focus on anything requiring memory. All at once she crashed to the floor, knocking over her small gardening caddy and scattering tools in every direction.

She tried to get up but could only manage to roll over on her back. *Is this it?* she asked herself. After all she'd been through as an agent, this was how she was going to die? Then she saw a white light coming from the six-inch-square window in the door and wondered if it was what so many people who approached death had reported. She fell back and let her eyes slide shut. Even with her mouth closed, she could taste the thick fumes in her throat.

The actual source of the light was a small flashlight held by a man standing outside, dressed in black. When she collapsed, he turned it off and pulled the two wedges from under the door that had jammed it closed against her efforts. Then he went to the front door of the residence and removed two more. Calmly, he put his hands in his pockets and walked back to a waiting SUV.

Lying there felt pleasant, euphoric, but then it occurred to Kate that the light was gone. Shouldn't it be inside her head, too? She opened her eyes, and it was still gone. Did that mean the death sentence had been revoked, or at least delayed? Whatever it meant, she decided that she was going down swinging.

Next to her was a rake, its wooden handle thick and straight. Pushing up on all fours, she crawled to the rear of the car, dragging the rake behind her. The fumes were completely suffocating. She peeled off one of her slippers with its thin rubber sole and crammed it into the tailpipe. She was familiar enough with cars to know that the obstruction alone wouldn't stop the engine as the movies depicted but would eventually be blown out by mounting pressure. So she stuck the rake's handle into the tailpipe, forcing the slipper even farther into the exhaust.

Then she maneuvered the wooden shaft, finally wedging the steel raking tines against one of the patterned grooves in the overhead garage door, which was a foot and a half away. One of two things would happen now: Either the pressure would build up and kill the engine or the rake would blow a hole in the door and provide fresh air. One or the other could save her. Of course, it was more likely that the handle of the rake would simply snap. She reached up and held the rake in place before crumpling to the floor to wait.

Something with a sharp edge was underneath her. She realized it was a gardening trowel that had been knocked across the floor when she first fell. Inching closer to the garage door, she shoved it under the rubber cleat that sealed the entire length of the door and, using both hands, turned it up on edge to make a small triangular opening. Placing her mouth as close to it as possible, she breathed in the sweet, cold, late-autumn air.

Just before she passed out, her hand slipped off the rake and she thought she heard the car's engine sputter and die.

AFTER CLIMBING INTO the backseat of the SUV, the man in black nodded to the two men in the front that it was done.

The driver, in his early fifties, was tall and slender, his suit expensive and American. His hair was full and carefully cut. His face might have been described as elegant if it weren't for the splayed, crooked nose, which gave his appearance a vague warning of violence. He looked over at the man sitting next to him to see if he was satisfied.

The passenger reached over and turned off the radio-signal device that had jammed Kate's remote-control door opener, the limited markings on it written in Cyrillic. He, too, was tall but powerfully built, and his age was difficult to estimate; he could have been in his fifties or in his sixties. His hands were thick and crisscrossed with dozens of thin white scars. His face was drawn and slightly exhausted, his eyes irreparably sad. Although his skin appeared a permanent gray, his lips were thick and an unusual shade of dark red. He looked back at the driver with eyes that never seemed to move from side to side. It was as if they were frozen in their sockets, making whomever he was talking to feel that turning away would be perceived as evasive, even when telling the truth. He searched the driver's face for any indication that he and his man hadn't been successful and then leaned his head back on the headrest and closed his eyes. The SUV pulled away from the curb.

KATE BANNON OPENED her eyes and wondered if she was dreaming again. Bob Lasker, the director of the FBI, sat next to her hospital bed. Struggling to recall what had happened, she wasn't sure she really could. "Am I dreaming?" she asked loudly, almost as if trying to determine if she was actually awake. She went to scratch her nose but then realized that an oxygen tube was pinching her nostrils.

"This is real, Kate." The director smiled warmly. "You gave us a scare, though. But you're going to be all right."

"I remember being in the garage and not being able to get out."

"One of your neighbors was taking his dog for a late-night walk, and I guess in the cool air he smelled the exhaust from the opening you made. He dragged his owner closer, and then the guy broke in, dragged you out, and called 911. Any idea how you left your car on?"

She told him about being bought a drink and not feeling well, then waking up to find her car running and not being able to get out of the garage. "I can't imagine doing that. And then locking the car door with the keys in the ignition? Who locks a car that's in a locked garage?"

"And this guy who bought you the drink, you never saw him before."

"Not that I remember. I would have remembered him from headquarters. He was nice-looking."

"Maybe he was just someone at the bar and saw a pretty girl."

"Maybe," she said vaguely, her mind searching for other possibilities.

Lasker stared at her as though there were some question he wasn't asking.

"What?" she demanded.

"Kate, don't take this the wrong way, but have you been feeling okay lately?"

She gave a short laugh. "Wait a minute—are you asking me if I've been depressed?"

"Yes."

She thought for a moment. "You think I tried to kill myself?"

The question was asked with such self-assurance that Lasker couldn't help but say, "No, I don't."

"But others do?"

"A deputy assistant director almost dies, there are questions that have to be considered."

"Meaning what?"

"OPR is going to look into it. Very routine, very low-key."

"I didn't try to commit suicide."

"You know I can't call off procedure. I wouldn't for any other agent, and since everyone knows how much I think of you, I can't in this instance either." He smiled. "Please cooperate and try not to shoot any of them. As soon as you feel well enough to get out of here, you'll be returned to full duty while they conduct their investigation."

"This is ridiculous."

"I know it is. If it does get to be too much, come and see me." Lasker patted her on the arm. "For now, get well. Everything else will take care of itself."

She was staring down at her hands but finally looked at him. "I guess I should be thanking you instead of arguing."

"Just get better, Kate."

Soon after the director left the room, an agent

whom Kate recognized as being from the Office of Professional Responsibility came in. "Hi, Kate. I'm Roger Daniels from OPR. How are you feeling?"

"Nonsuicidal."

He laughed. "I know this is a lot coming at you all at once. I can wait to take your statement."

Kate sat up and took a sip of water from a cup on the table next to her bed. "Don't be *too* offended, but the sooner we get started, the sooner I'll have OPR out of my life."

The agent chuckled. "Well, that carbon monoxide didn't damage your sense of humor."

"Who said I was trying to be funny? Roger, I'm sure you're a very capable agent, and maybe even a nice guy, but I did a stint at OPR, so please don't waste any of the artificial sweeteners on me. Just ask me your questions, and I'll give you my best answers."

"Fair enough, Kate." He opened his notebook. "Did you attempt suicide?" His tone was noticeably less friendly.

"I'm the one who stopped the car engine and wedged a trowel under the door to save myself. Does that sound like I was trying to commit suicide?"

"It's not uncommon during a suicide attempt for people to have a change of heart. They take pills and then call 911. Move the gun at the last moment and just wound themselves. It happens more frequently than you think."

"Yeah, well, I happen to like my life quite a bit."

"Don't take this the wrong way, but some people do it for attention."

"How could I possibly take that the wrong way?"

she said, sounding more than a little sarcastic. She took a moment and then said, "If you knew me, you'd know I really don't care what people think. Why would I want to get their attention?"

"Not people—*person*," he said.

"Person? Who?"

The agent flipped back to another page in his notes. "Steve Vail?"

"Where did you get that?"

"Answers, Kate, remember?"

"Okay, what do you know about him? And me?"

"We know that he was fired as an agent more than five years ago. That the director brought him back to work on the Rubaco Pentad case in Los Angeles—with you—and that you guys have dated. Recently it ended abruptly."

"Sounds like you got a running start on this while I was still unconscious. Okay, I'll tell you about Vail on one condition—that you don't contact him."

"If you're forthcoming, there'll be no need to."

"One of the hardest things I've had to do in my life was tell him I didn't want him in it. If you've read the Pentad file, you know he was responsible for solving that case almost single-handedly. He would be an incredible agent, but he cannot conform to anything, and that includes a relationship with me. We've seen each other three times since L.A. The first time was—I hate to use the word, but it was—pretty much perfect. The last two were absolutely awful. So I told him it would be best if we didn't see each other again. And that was a week ago. So no, I wasn't trying to get his attention."

"Trying to find out exactly who he was, I ran his name through some of our contacts at other agencies and got a hit with the State Department. Seems you and he are going to the Irish ambassador's reception on New Year's Eve."

"Boy, you have been busy. But you'd better check with them again. It should show that my escort is now Eamon Walsh."

"So you changed it."

"What's today?"

"Wednesday."

"I spoke with him Monday. He's with the Irish embassy and was the one who called me originally with the invitation. When I phoned him back to tell him Vail wasn't coming, he asked if I'd do him the honor. I didn't want to go alone, so I said yes. Maybe he hasn't gotten around to changing it officially yet. You can call him."

Daniels was making notes. "So it's definitely over between you and Vail. You told him not to come for New Year's Eve."

"Not in so many words, but I think 'We shouldn't see each other again' carries that assumption."

"That's helpful about Vail. It gives you one less reason to . . . you know."

"Off myself."

"Tell me what you remember about the night that this happened to you," Daniels said.

She repeated what she'd told the director about the stranger's buying her a drink that didn't settle well with her, then her coming home and going to bed. Then waking up and trying to get out of the garage.

He asked, "You said he told you it was Drambuie?"

"Yes."

"Hmm," Daniels said more to himself than to her.

"What?"

"I've had Drambuie, and it has a definite strong sweetness to it."

The OPR agent started making additional notes that she guessed were more than just about Kate's response. As she watched him, she remembered her time in OPR, how investigations were not about the incident but about the employee's involvement in it. They weren't criminal investigators, they were personnel investigators. As Daniels looked up from his pad ready to ask the next question, she knew that he was not going to get to the bottom of this. If anyone was going to find out what had happened, it would have to be her. "If that guy did put something in the drink, maybe he had some other intentions, and when he saw I drank only one sip of it, he got scared and took off."

"Your blood didn't show any kind of drug in it, but if you didn't drink much, maybe it dissipated before you got here."

"Are you going to try to track him down?" she asked, trying to judge just how far he was going to pursue what had happened to her.

"I'll have to see where everything takes me."

Right, she said to herself, becoming lost in thought. There was just something about a near-death experience that brought Vail to mind. And she couldn't decide whether that was a good thing or a bad thing. She knew that he would never just "see where everything takes me." A small smile creased her lips.

"What is it, Kate?"

"Oh, no, nothing. Did you need anything else?"

"That's enough for now." Daniels stood up. "Take care."

He closed the door, and after a moment her smile disappeared.

She was sure she was never going to see Vail again.

ONE

KATE BANNON OPENED HER DOOR. "WHAT ARE YOU DOING here?"

With mock surprise on his face, Steve Vail recoiled slightly at the level of protest in her voice. He stepped inside, setting down his suitcase and, for the briefest moment, allowed his eyes to trace the flawless symmetry of her face. "I've got the right day, don't I? This is New Year's Eve. Is it the wrong year?"

"After that last time, when I told you this wasn't going to work, I assumed you understood that included tonight."

He smiled crookedly. "Come on, Kate, it's the twenty-first century. What woman wants to have to admit that she's never been stalked? It's become an accoutrement, like Italian shoes or one of those little purse-size dogs."

"We tried, Steve. Three times. And the last two, if you remember, were not pretty."

"That means statistically we're due."

Kate shook her head slowly. She really couldn't believe he was standing there. "You know as well as I do that we're a disaster. We're too different. Or too much alike. I don't know. Every time we try to get close, we wind up driving each other crazy. You don't know how much I wanted it to work, but it can't."

Vail looked at her dress. "I guess you were planning to go to whatever this was tonight without me. Why don't we go together and see what happens? What's the worst that can happen? So I ruin your career. That would probably be the best thing that could happen to us."

"I have to go to this. It's a command performance. And you know exactly what it is—an ambassador's reception. Why else would you have a suit on? Even though the proper dress is a tuxedo. Which I'm going to guess was your way of letting all the *phonies* in the room know that you're a lowly bricklayer."

"A man has to seek amusement wherever he can."

"I'll never understand you. You could be whatever you want. You have advanced degrees. The director has offered you complete autonomy if you'll come back to the Bureau, but instead you choose physical labor just so you won't have to take orders. If that's who you are, fine, but you don't get to rub everyone else's face in it simply because they're not like you." She looked at him sternly. "It's called hypocrisy." She could see that her words had stung him, but she couldn't find anything inaccurate in what she'd said.

He reached up and traced the small L-shaped scar high on her cheekbone and then smiled gently. "You don't have to wonder anymore, Kate, whether we're too much alike. There was a time, and not very long ago, that you would have thought they were phonies, too," he said. "But you're right, I've been a phony myself. The only defense I can offer is that you make my compass go haywire. The only reason I'm doing any of this is you."

He turned and opened the door. "Like you said, we gave it a shot," he said. "When it was right, it was like nothing I've ever experienced. That's why I had to try one last time."

"You can't just walk out like that. Not after everything we've been through."

"*This* is the best way to leave it. Then we won't have any lingering doubts."

"At least let me drive you to the airport. It's freezing out."

"I live in Chicago, remember? This isn't cold."

"I'll feel better about this if I can take you. It'll give us a chance to talk a little more. Right now I feel like we're supposed to hate each other."

"It'll be fine, Kate. I'll get a taxi."

"It's New Year's Eve—you'll never find one."

"You're probably right." He picked up his suitcase. "Okay, I'll take a ride, but only if we don't talk. I don't want to say anything that'll make this worse."

For the briefest moment, she considered telling him about the night before Thanksgiving and asking him what he thought about the guy in the bar. The day she got home from the hospital, she'd gone into her garage to change the battery in the remote for the overhead door. But it had worked fine. She thought that maybe she'd just pushed the wrong part of it in her semiconscious state. But three days ago she'd realized that it had been over a month and she hadn't heard anything from OPR.

So she'd gone back into the garage and retraced the events from that night as best she could. That's when she realized that she couldn't have opened the inside door to her condominium if her keys were locked in the car.

Then she'd bought a bottle of Drambuie and tasted it. It had a honey-sweet taste to it, nothing like what she remembered from the bar.

The next day she'd checked with the Metropolitan Police, and they'd said they hadn't had any recent drug-facilitated rapes reported. Since she was sneaking around behind OPR's back, she didn't want to start asking questions of people who were at the bar and have it get back to Daniels. Vail, who saw these things on a different level, would have been the perfect person to ask. But under the circumstances, giving him a reason to stay would be counterproductive.

"If that's the way you want to leave this," she said.

The phone rang. "You'd better get that," he said. "The Bureau probably thought we actually had a date and needed to ruin it one last time."

"That isn't fair."

"Probably not, but you can't say it's inaccurate."

"This is exactly why it would never work between us. Not everyone who takes orders for a living is a mortal enemy of Steven Vail."

Vail held up his hands in apology. "I told you I'd say something that would make it worse."

As she walked to the phone, she decided to lighten the mood and try to initiate some sort of interim peace. "I know it's been a while since the FBI fired you, but nobody gets called out on Thanksgiving,

Christmas, or New Year's Eve. It's in our latest contract." She picked up the receiver. "Kate Bannon. Oh, hi, Tim. Happy New Year." She listened and after a few seconds turned her back to Vail.

He sat down on his suitcase and waited for the inevitable change of plans.

She hung up and said, "A seven-year-old boy was abducted in Reston, Virginia, which is two towns over from here."

When she didn't offer any other details, he said, "The FBI doesn't have jurisdiction for twenty-four hours in an abduction. Why did they call you?"

"The Reston chief is a retired agent from the Washington Field Office. We go back a lot of years. He's a good guy, but something like this, he's probably in over his head. His entire career was working applicant cases, asking the same handful of questions about character and loyalty. Would you mind if we stopped there on the way? It shouldn't take long. He just needs some reassurance—you know, what help the Bureau can give him. Maybe a little direction."

In a cryptic tone, Vail said, "I wouldn't miss it for the world."

"You wouldn't miss what?" she asked suspiciously.

"You pretending not to get involved to prove to me, and yourself, that your career isn't what's come between us."

"If you're trying to ensure that there'll be no talking on the way, congratulations." She handed him her keys. "There's one more call I have to make, would you mind warming up the car?"

Vail gave her an inquiring look and then started

laughing. "No wonder you're able to resist my charms. You have a date."

"It's not actually a—"

Vail held up his hands. "Kate, it's fine. I was hoping you weren't serious about it being over. That's why I came. Obviously I was wrong. I'll go start the car."

Five minutes later Kate walked into the garage and climbed behind the wheel. As soon as they pulled out, Vail asked, "How long has the boy been gone?"

"So we *are* going to talk."

"I'm just trying to establish the parameters of your *momentary* detour."

"Why?"

"So I'll be able to mark the exact second you violated the estimate of your involvement."

"You really think you've got me figured out, don't you?"

"Not that it matters anymore, but oh yeah," Vail answered.

She turned to him, wanting to look indignant but knowing she couldn't pull it off. Then she told him, "Tim said about five hours."

"You do understand that the chances of him being found alive are not good."

"Then I guess you do understand that's why I have to go."

Vail stared straight ahead for a moment. "I do."

KATE FLASHED HER credentials at the police officer behind the glass, and he opened the door for her and Vail. They were led to a small conference room where more than a dozen police officers and detectives sat crowded around a conference table designed for half that number.

The chief, Tim Mallon, rose anxiously and shook hands with her. She introduced him to Vail. One of the officers got up so Kate could sit down and Vail backed up against the closest wall.

Mallon handed Kate a sheet of paper and a photo. "That's the boy, Joey Walton, and the BOLO we put out along with the Amber Alert. He and his parents were at a local New Year's Eve 5K run. It also had a half-mile race for the kids. The parents watched the start, and by the time they got to the finish line, he was gone. No one's seen him since."

Kate said, "Okay, Tim, what can the Bureau do for you?"

"I was hoping you could tell me. Obviously, we could use a profiler and anything else along those lines you can think of."

"As soon as we're done here, I'll make some calls. I assume you're looking into registered sex offenders in the area."

The chief nodded at a detective sitting halfway around the table, who said, "I'm expecting a list any minute."

"I guess that's going to be the best lead for now."

"What else?" Mallon asked.

"Put out a plea to the media, along with the boy's photo."

"That's been done, Kate. And we have the parents doing interviews, trying to personalize the boy for whoever took him," Mallon said. "Isn't there anything else we can do?"

"Sometimes you just have to give the public some time to respond. There's a chance somebody knows who did this."

"I'm sorry, I don't want to sit and wait. There must be something we can do to be more proactive. What would you do if it were a Bureau case?"

She hesitated a moment, glancing back at Vail. "Tim, I'm sorry. I've never worked kidnappings, but I can make some calls and see if we can get someone out here from the Washington Field Office."

Mallon looked confused. "Kate, I spent twenty years at WFO. If I thought someone there had the answer, I wouldn't have called you." He looked around the men at the table, hoping someone would offer an idea of what to do next.

Kate said, "I misjudged what you needed, Tim." Then she got up and, with an apologetic grin to him, handed Vail the photo and the BOLO. "How about it, Steve? Can you give them a hand?"

Somewhat surprised, the chief said, "I'm sorry, Steve, are you with the Bureau?"

"Actually, I'm a bricklayer. From Chicago." He handed the items back to Kate. "In fact, I'm on my way back there now."

Mallon shot a confused look at Kate. "Steve's a former agent who has helped us in the past. Take my word, right now you want him in the room."

"Sorry, Steve," Mallon said. "You're both dressed up. I thought you were just Kate's date."

Vail smiled disarmingly. "Funny how easy it is to make that assumption."

Sensing some rift between the two of them, the chief said, "Steve, if you can help, we'd be grateful. This is a seven-year-old boy's life we're talking about."

Vail pushed himself off the wall with obvious reluctance, his eyes locked onto Kate's, purposely without emotion. "Sure." Vail looked around the table. "Any of you ever work a child kidnapping by a stranger before?" One older uniformed officer raised his hand unconvincingly. Vail took a moment to consider something. "Chief, I'd recontact all the media outlets and have them put out a plea for help from anyone at the race. It being a kids' run, a lot of people are going to be taking pictures with both their cameras and their cell phones. Ask everyone to immediately e-mail all their photos to the station. Every one of them, whether they think they're connected or not." Kate watched as Vail became silent, lost in some other thought. "I assume that race officials also took photos. Have them do the same, including those from the adult race. Have you gotten a list of runners from them?"

The chief pointed at one of the detectives, who said, "They're supposed to be forwarding it."

"You'll want that right now. Also from the kids' race," Vail said. "That it's a holiday and twice as hard for the police to get anything done may not be a coincidence. Whoever's responsible for this may have learned by past mistakes. As in *convicted* child molester. Which, as Kate suggested, makes the sex-offenders list a top priority."

"What else?" Mallon asked.

Vail stepped forward to better engage the men around the table. "I know everybody is trying to think positive, but after this amount of time, statistically, there's only a slightly better-than-even chance that the boy is still alive. Not a pleasant thought, but you're police officers—you're paid to approach things from a clinical and, maybe more important, a cynical perspective. There's also a fifty-percent chance the boy's been sexually assaulted. And the longer this goes, the worse those odds become. So if cars are stopped or your instinct tells you to search someplace, don't get it in your mind that you're going to hear the victim pounding on doors or walls to be freed. Assume you're looking for a body. And remember, in a situation like this—I'm sorry, Chief—it's better to do something that's wrong than it is to do nothing at all. If someone won't allow you access, politely search anyway. Just remember: Be polite and explain the situation. Whoever took the boy is one of the few people who won't cooperate in an instance like this."

Mallon stood up and addressed his officers. "Don't any of you worry about liability. Like Steve said, explain, be polite, and then do what you have to do. All the heat is on me." To Kate and Vail, he said, "We've already got more than thirty tips. The media has been running the story every half hour. Each time they do, we get more. We're going to start chasing them down." He turned back to the officers and detectives around the table. "Any questions?" There were none. "Okay, I'll be here. If you run into anyone who's reluctant to help, and there's time, call me and I'll make the decision." The officers got up and started filing out. "Kate, you can use my office to make those calls."

"Okay."

"Steve, can I ask you to give us a hand with the tips? Sounds like you know what to look for. Maybe you'll see something we're missing."

"If I can get one of your people to run me to the airport when we're through. Kate's already late for something she needs to get to."

"Sure." Mallon glanced at her. "Kate, if you need to go, I'll understand."

Kate could tell that Vail hadn't said it maliciously. "It's nothing that can't wait, Tim. And if I don't make it, it's not a big deal. I'm here because we're friends. I'll stay until you don't need me any longer."

Vail said, "Chief, if you have a desk somewhere with a computer, I'll start on those tips. And a map of the area if you have one."

"Great. And I'll make sure you get copies of anything new that comes in."

Kate said, "Tim, could you give us a minute?"

"Sure." Mallon walked out and shut the door.

She put her hand on his arm. "I appreciate your keeping me from looking like a fool."

"No use both of us feeling that way."

She started to say something, and he placed his hand over hers. "It's okay, Bannon." He leaned forward and whispered in her ear. "I really do hate New Year's Eve parties."

He turned to go, and she said, "And don't think you can sneak out of here without saying good-bye."

Vail gave her a silent but formal salute.

While Kate started making phone calls, trying to track down agents from the Behavioral Science Unit and the Washington Field Office, the chief led Vail to a detective's desk and showed him how to access the department's different databases. He settled in and started reading the tips.

Unlike the officers and detectives, Vail had the luxury of looking at them from a different perspective. The Reston Police Department had to investigate all the tips offered. Vail didn't. So he was able to start making judgments about the callers and the individuals they were reporting on.

He checked each suspect's name in the computer to see if there were any previous contacts with the department. He also checked the callers' names—if they gave one—to see if they were chronic complaint makers, which could lessen the priority of their information. After reading all the tips, he hadn't found any he considered worthwhile. That wasn't necessarily a bad thing. Tips were a double-edged sword. While they frequently solved a case, a false lead that looked promising could be distracting, take the entire department in the wrong direction, and burn precious time. A uniformed officer walked in and asked, "You Vail?"

He stood up and shook hands. "Steve, yes."

The policeman put three more tips on the pile. "These are from the last half hour. We're also starting to get photos from the races e-mailed in. Do you want me to forward them to this computer?"

"I'd appreciate it." Vail picked up the newest tips. "Anything interesting?"

"Nothing we'll need lights and sirens for."

Vail continued searching the names through the computer. Still nothing jumped out at him. When he finished, he got up and wandered around until he found someone who directed him to a coffeepot. He filled two cups and went looking for Kate.

The chief's office was small but well ordered. Bureau memorabilia neatly lined the wall behind the desk. Kate was on the phone, so Vail placed the cup in front of her and sat down.

She rolled her eyes as she listened to the latest excuse as to why nothing could be done tonight, taking a sip of coffee. He watched her and was reminded of one of the things that he liked most about her: She thrived on work. The more difficult the case, the more focused she became. He listened as she urged cooperation. Her tone was compelling, and Vail couldn't tell whether it was actually cajoling or threatening or both. Finally she hung up midsentence. "Come January second, there'll be a number of Bureau employees who are going to be at least as unhappy as I am right now."

"Makes me almost sorry I won't be here."

She gave him a small, sad smile through pursed lips and leaned back in her chair. "Anything in the tips?"

"Not so far. The photos are starting to come in, though."

"Do you actually think we'd get that lucky?"

"I just thought it would be better to have them than not. You never know, something could come up later that a photo might help with," Vail said. "And the pendulum is due to swing the other way."

"What pendulum?"

"What most people call luck. To me it's nothing

more than a temporary statistical aberration. So far tonight I've had an unbelievable amount of bad luck, so maybe I'm due."

"Sorry." She stared at him for a moment before taking another sip of coffee. "Do you know what I find to be the most confounding thing about you, Steve?"

"That doesn't sound like a question a judicious person would want to hear the answer to."

"That you're so good at this and refuse to do it for a living."

"Don't start."

The chief knocked on the door and came in. "Sorry. We may have something. From the sex-offenders list, there's one, a Frank Dillon, who kidnapped and molested a six-year-old boy twelve years ago. He was paroled in September, and he lives in Vienna, which is fairly close. We got ahold of his parole officer, who said Dillon recently changed his residence and stopped reporting. As far as the PO is concerned, he's AWOL, and he'll violate him if we want. We just made a call to his last employment, and he was at work until noon today, when he just up and quit. He did leave a cell-phone number so they could call him when his last check was ready. We're going to try to put the grab on him. You guys want to come along?"

"Sure," Kate said. She looked at Vail.

"You won't need me, Chief. I'm a civilian. If something happened, my being there would just give some defense attorney a little more smoke to blind a jury with. Besides, somebody should stay here and keep checking on the tips in case this guy doesn't work out."

Kate turned to the chief. "Tim, I'm coming with you. I'll be there in a minute." Once Mallon left, she said, "I seem to remember something about you always keeping the best lead for yourself. That's not what this is, is it?"

"Like the chief said before, we're talking about a child's life."

"Sorry." She took out her car keys. "When's the last time you ate?"

"Ah . . . breakfast."

"Please go get something. Those tips won't miss you for fifteen minutes. And I really do appreciate this, Steve," she said. "Hopefully, this won't take long. *Hopefully*, this is our guy."

When Vail got back to the detective's desk, there were four new tip sheets. He checked the e-mails and was surprised to see that the department had already received eleven messages with photos attached. The lists of runners for both races had also been forwarded. He opened the first set of pictures; they were all of the adult race. He scanned the faces, looking for the Walton boy. There was a subtle difference in quality between the phone pictures and those taken with cameras. As long as they didn't have to be blown up to provide detail, it really didn't matter.

Because of the cold weather, most of the runners were bundled up, especially the children. The kids' race seemed more crowded, with all those parents waiting at the finish line. Vail went through them three times, trying to spot Joey Walton. According to the runners' list, the sandy-haired seven-year-old was number 034. There were a couple of possibilities that looked like him physically, but the numbers pinned to their chests indicated otherwise.

An angry knot of frustration turned in Vail's stomach, and he started to regret not going with Kate. The fugitive pedophile sounded like a decent lead. If it wasn't him, Frank Dillon had certainly picked an odd time to stop reporting to his parole officer and disappear. By staying behind, Vail knew he was trying to make something happen, create some insightful discovery. Apparently he did miss the chase, but at the moment it seemed little more than useless self-indulgence. Or maybe he just wanted to impress Kate.

He started to get up to refill his coffee when the e-mail tone sounded again. There were three new messages, which had eight additional photographs attached. He took his time and looked through them twice. Then, realizing that he had no idea what he was looking for, he got to his feet and waved at the monitor in disgust. He was trying to look at the case from too many angles, a sure way to not find anything.

Outside the department's front door, he stood without a coat, trying to use the cold to redirect his thoughts. He stayed there until he could feel the bite of the wind, letting the discomfort distract him from his failing approach to the investigation.

Then one of the latest photos flashed through his mind. But the image did not last long enough for him to figure out why it had risen out of his subconscious. He hurried back to the desk and pulled the picture up on the screen. After studying every little detail, he still couldn't see anything. He closed his eyes and then slammed his fist on the desk.

The image was that of a boy, about eleven years old, breaking the tape at the children's race. There were a number of adults standing on the sidelines looking back up the course, trying to find their children in the onrushing pack. It was crowded, and people were walking in all directions. Vail could see how easy it would be to lure a seven-year-old away without anyone's noticing. By the race numbers pinned to their chests, Vail could see that some of the adults had competed in the 5K run, while the rest were apparently just observers. Then he saw what he had missed.

One of the adult runners seemed to be looking at the camera as if he were measuring its danger. His arm was in front of his number so it couldn't be read. Vail couldn't tell if he was blocking it intentionally. But what he'd initially missed was that there was a smaller square of paper attached to the lower left corner of the man's race number. It had been safety-pinned on so it could be collected at the end of the 3.1-mile race to document finish place and time. Unfortunately, because of the angle, Vail couldn't make it out either. The man was dark-complected and burly, not a runner's build. Most people who would run in the cold air of New Year's Eve were probably not novices. That the number tag was still there suggested he had not run the adult race. His registering could have been a ruse calculated to get him close to the children without seeming suspicious.

The e-mail tone sounded again, and Vail glanced at the monitor. It was from the race officials. Attached were all of their photos. Still lost in thought, Vail ignored it, trying to find a way to determine if the individual in the photo was involved in the boy's disappearance. Then it hit him. The photo was taken the moment the race's winner was crossing the finish line. Logically, the official pictures would cover that moment and then beyond.

Quickly, he opened the e-mail and began studying the images. The first twenty or so were of the adult race. He looked for that same individual, thinking the man might have initially been in that area. Vail couldn't find him. Then the chronologically sequenced photos started documenting the beginning of the children's run. Vail carefully searched each of them. He knew what the man was wearing and was hoping for a clear shot of his number, which he could match to the runners' list. There was another one of the young man winning, but Vail's suspect was not in it.

A half-dozen photographs later, there was one of a man in the distance who appeared to be the right size and with the same clothing as in the earlier photo. He had his back to the camera and stood next to a van. Vail couldn't tell whether he was stopped there or walking by. The van's plate was visible, but it was too distant to make out.

Vail found the computer's Photoshop program and opened it, pulling up the picture. Because the image had been taken with a quality camera, the pixel density was high and allowed him to blow up the license plate to where it could be read. He made a note of it and then centered the photo on the individual. In the space between the man's legs, unseen before, was what looked like the leg of a child wearing red pants. Vail called the dispatcher and had her run the van's plate.

While he waited, he shuffled through the growing stack of pages on the desk until he found the BOLO that had been sent out originally. Joey Walton was last seen wearing a black hooded sweatshirt and red sweatpants. The dispatcher came back on the line and advised that the plate came back to a George Hillstrand with a Herndon, Virginia, address.

Vail found Hillstrand's name on the adult race roster and then checked him in the Reston PD computer. Four years earlier, he had evidently worked in Reston, because the department had gotten a call about him from the Maryland State Police, who were conducting an investigation of a child who had disappeared in Colesville, Maryland. They had called to see if Reston had had any previous contact with Hillstrand. They hadn't.

The seven-year-old, Edward Stanton, had disappeared during a party at one of those pizza-and-game places that specialized in letting the kids run all over while the parents drank pitcher beer and doled out tokens to keep them busy. Hillstrand's name had somehow come up in their investigation, but no specifics were listed.

Vail called the dispatcher again and had her run Edward Stanton's name to see if the boy, or his body, had ever been found. After a short wait, she told him that the missing-person notice in NCIC was still active. Vail asked for the boy's description. It was not unusual for serial offenders to seek victims who were physically similar. The two boys' ages when kidnapped were close. She said, "At the time of incident, he was seven years old, four feet one inch tall, and weighed sixty pounds. Medium-brown hair, blue eyes. Under distinguishing marks, he has a crescent-shaped scar on the crown of his head." A lot of things were matching up, but Vail had seen it before. "Proof positive" that turned out to be a series of impossible coincidences but were in fact just that.

With time so critical, the lead had to be checked out now. He found the dispatcher's office and went in. "Hi, I'm Steve Vail. How're they doing?"

Before she could answer, a request to run a plate came over the air. She turned to the computer to type it in and said, "They're sitting on three places right now, waiting for this guy to come back. Did you want me to tell them something?"

"No, they've got their hands full. I'll catch up with them later." Vail also knew that if he waited for them, investigative protocol would have to be followed. First, the Maryland State Police would have to be contacted to see if Hillstrand was actually a suspect in the case or, instead, if his name had come up as the result of some other "shotgun" approach, which was not unusual in that kind of case. Hundreds, even thousands of names could be generated and never be fully investigated because of sheer volume. The fact that the state police had never followed up with a more detailed query indicated that Hillstrand was probably not a strong suspect at the time. And in all likelihood, due to the holiday, specific details from the MSP probably wouldn't be available until sometime tomorrow at the earliest. Then, if Hillstrand had been a suspect in the Maryland abduction and somehow could be shown to be involved in the Walton boy's disappearance, a prosecutor would have to be contacted for a search warrant while the police went out to surveil Hillstrand's residence. And finally, finding an accommodating judge on New Year's Day might prove to be a small miracle in itself. By then, in all probability, it would be too late.

Or Vail could just go there now and have a look for himself.

He opened the drawers to the desk he'd been working at to see if the detective kept a backup weapon. The only thing he found was an extra badge with a clip-on backing. He snapped it onto his belt and left Kate a note, telling her he'd gone to check out Hillstrand, along with the address and how Hillstrand's name had surfaced. Although the information should prevent her from accusing him of hiding leads, he knew how she would interpret it. He added a P.S.: *"This is a long shot, so I didn't want to bother you with it."* He reread it and shook his head. The only way that he wasn't going to be accused of deception was if Hillstrand was one of those false leads in which only Vail's time had been wasted.

In the parking lot, Vail opened the trunk, hoping that Kate's Bureau car might have been equipped with a shotgun. It wasn't. He got in, started the engine, and pulled out into the light traffic.

There was an advantage to not involving Kate

or any of the Reston PD. As long as he acted on his own, as a non-law-enforcement citizen, he had greater latitude for gathering evidence without a search warrant than sworn officers did, especially if the police didn't know what he was doing. If they did, then he could be legally considered an agent of the department. In fact, under these circumstances his room to maneuver was almost limitless. While the exigent circumstances of a young boy's life could mitigate violations of the Fourth Amendment, Vail was still worried that a pedophile might escape justice because the drafters of the Constitution hadn't foreseen the downward-spiraling depravity at the fringes of the American male population. At least that would have been his explanation if it weren't for Kate. She'd heard all his rhetoric for working alone before. In fact, it had created an almost irreparable rift between them the only other time they'd worked together. But at the moment it looked like she was, at best, his ride to the airport, so why not?

Glancing at the map again, he turned down a street and watched as the houses became more and more isolated. It then became an unpaved road that disappeared into the woods.

Vail came to a stop and lifted his foot from the brake, allowing the vehicle to advance at idle speed. It was another fifty yards before he saw any lights. He stopped again and switched off the engine. The car was still hidden by the thick evergreen woods. He got out and walked quietly toward the house. It was a single-level dwelling and bigger than Vail thought would be built in such a remote location.

He walked around the tree line at the edge of

the clearing, trying to determine the exact size and layout of the structure. There were no outbuildings on the property, so if Hillstrand did have the boy, he had to be inside the house. As quietly as possible, Vail hurried back to the car, started it, and drove up to the house. The older paneled van from the photo was parked in front. Enough lights were on inside to indicate that someone was home.

Vail got out, walked directly to the front door, and knocked. The exterior of the house needed paint, but the property immediately around it seemed fairly well maintained. A bright light overhead came on, and the man in the race photo opened the door. His eyes were dark like his hair—possibly Mediterranean, Vail thought. His stare never left Vail's as the two men sized each other up. Finally Hillstrand said, "Can I help you?"

Vail pulled the detective badge from his belt and held it up. "I'm with the Reston Police. Detective Vail. We're investigating a missing child. Do you have a minute?"

"Sure," he answered, and stepped back, inviting Vail in. Once he was inside, Hillstrand shut the door. "That's an awfully nice suit for a detective." His voice had a trace of suspicion in it. "Do you mind if I ask to see your photo ID?"

Vail patted his chest pockets as if looking for his identification. He then reached under his coat and searched his pants pockets. "Sorry, I don't have it with me. I'm afraid you caught me, Mr. Hillstrand. I was on my way to a party when I got the call. Didn't even get to go into the station. They just gave me some people to go and interview. The people who were at the race tonight where the boy disappeared. I don't know if you heard about it. We're hoping someone saw something."

"You must have been caught short. I can see you're not carrying a gun either."

"That's why they gave me just the people who were in the race, I guess. The friendlies. Any chance you saw anything?" Vail could hear the television on in another room. "I'm assuming you've seen it on TV."

Hillstrand didn't answer right away but instead stared at Vail as though contemplating something he'd said. "Yes, it's hard not to have. If I had any photographs, I would have sent them. And I'm sorry, I didn't see anything out of the ordinary. Not that I can remember."

"How'd you do on the run? Three miles is a fair distance."

Hillstrand smiled uneasily. "I finished. I'm not an avid runner, so my goals are modest."

"I don't know how modest three miles is. I don't think I could make it. Did you get over to see the children's run?"

Hillstrand hesitated, and Vail suspected that he remembered looking into the camera that had taken his photo. "It was on the way to where my van was parked, so I stopped and watched the winner finish."

The voice of a young boy came from another room. "Dad, who is it?"

"That your son?" Vail asked.

"Yes, it is." Hillstrand led the way into the living room. A boy whose age Vail guessed at ten or eleven sat on the couch watching TV. He had medium-brown hair and was at least a foot taller than Joey Walton was reported to be.

"David, this is Detective Vail from the Reston Police Department. He's investigating that missing boy from the race they keep talking about."

The boy stood up and offered his hand. "How do you do, sir."

Vail took it and looked into his pale blue eyes. "Your parents letting you stay up to bring in the New Year?"

"My dad is. My mom passed away when I was born, during childbirth." Vail noted that he pronounced the words mechanically, without any sadness, his language a little too mature to be his own. The boy pointed to a nearby shelf. "That's a picture of her with my dad." Again the words seemed practiced.

Vail looked at the obviously pregnant woman in the photo standing next to George Hillstrand. Her coloring was even darker than her husband's was, her eyes almost pitch-black. "I'm sorry, David. That's really tough. I lost my mom early in my life, too. I know how hard that can be." Vail reached up and tousled the boy's hair.

He pulled his hand back carefully so as to not reveal what he had discovered. It is genetically improbable that couples with brown eyes will have a child with blue eyes, and David's hair and skin were nowhere close to the darkness of his "parents'." When Vail ruffled the boy's hair, he felt the crescent-shaped scar on the crown of his head. Unbelievably, David had to be Edward Stanton, the child abducted four years earlier in Maryland.

Which meant that, in all likelihood, Joey Walton was somewhere in the house. Talk about the luck pendulum swinging in the other direction.

The boy started to sit down in front of the TV again when Hillstrand said, "That's enough for tonight, son. It's time for bed." Without any argument, the boy got up and said, "Good night, sir."

"Good night, David," Vail answered.

"Let me get him tucked in, Detective. I'll be right back. Please make yourself comfortable."

Vail went over to the photograph of Hillstrand and his wife and carefully examined it, trying to determine how old it was. By the clothing and the faded color of the picture, he guessed it was at least ten years old.

Suddenly Vail felt Hillstrand's presence behind him. He turned around and found Hillstrand holding a .45 automatic on him. "Four years and you're the first one to notice that his coloring didn't fit. I guess I should put away that picture of my wife. I keep it there for my son. It took a while, but now he remembers her as his mother."

"I was hoping you wouldn't notice me noticing."

"It's something I've always been afraid of. When you ran your hand through his hair, I knew."

"And Joey?"

"He's fine. Downstairs in a locked room. He'll be restricted until he learns he's better off here."

"Than with his parents?"

"Since I'm the one with the gun, you don't get to be judgmental," Hillstrand said. "Besides, if they were good parents, they wouldn't have left him alone in a crowd like that."

"You mean with the pedophiles and all."

Hillstrand raised the gun and pointed it at Vail's face. "I am not a pedophile."

Vail took a closer look at the gun and said, "That thing looks pretty old. Sure it still works?"

"It was my grandfather's and it works just fine."

"That particular model is military. It has a number of safeties. Are you sure it's set to fire?"

Hillstrand smiled. "I've shot it enough times since my father left it to me to be positive."

Vail was trying to determine how familiar Hillstrand was with the weapon. Because it had been designed for the military, it had four separate safeties. Not many people knew about the disconnector safety. If the end of the barrel could be pushed back a fraction of an inch toward the person holding the weapon, the hammer wouldn't release. Since Hillstrand didn't seem to know all that much about the mechanics of the gun, Vail thought if he could get into position and push it toward him—with the body's natural tendency to push back—it would keep the safety engaged for the split second it would take to disarm him.

But right now Hillstrand was standing just far enough away to prevent that. "Can you at least let me see the boy, then?" Vail asked.

"Sure. With the carpeting and all up here, it'll be less messy downstairs."

"Call me cynical, but that doesn't sound like a very happy New Year to me."

Hillstrand's only response was to wave the gun toward the basement door. Once they were downstairs, he pointed to a heavy steel door with a thick lock and hasp. "He's in there." Carefully he tossed Vail the keys. Vail opened the lock and turned back to Hillstrand, holding the keys in his outstretched right hand. Hillstrand took a cautious step closer. Vail knew that this was it.

As Hillstrand reached for the key ring, Vail half turned back to the door and, appearing distracted, drew the key ring back about six inches. Hillstrand leaned slightly forward to get it. Vail spun quickly and stepped into him, placing his hand over the muzzle of the gun and pushing it into Hillstrand.

For a split second, Hillstrand pushed back against Vail's hand, pulling at the frozen trigger frantically. But as Vail turned to get a better grip on the weapon, Hillstrand drew it back and pulled the trigger. The .45's explosion echoed slowly through the basement.

KATE AND THE Reston chief, Tim Mallon, sat behind his desk watching the interrogation of their sex-offender suspect, Frank Dillon, on a closed-circuit monitor. "What do you think, Kate, is it him?"

She watched the suspect's body language closely. "It's hard to tell with these sociopaths. And I'm certainly no expert. I promise you that someone from Behavioral Sciences will be up here tomorrow. This detective seems to know what he's doing, though. As soon as Vail gets back, he may be able to figure it out."

"Where is he? The desk officer said he went out."

"I think he went to get something to eat."

There was a knock at the door. A uniformed officer stepped in. "Chief, the parents are here."

"Bring them back." Mallon turned off the monitor.

"You want me to leave, Tim?" Kate asked.

"God, no. That the FBI is involved is the most reassuring thing I can tell them right now."

The door opened again, and Mr. and Mrs. Walton walked in. Mallon introduced them both to Kate, and everyone sat down. Confusion and grief distorted Mrs. Walton's face. Her makeup and hair were disheveled. Her husband, whose eyes were slightly red, tried to strike a calmer pose, more to keep his wife's teetering hysteria in check than as a reflection of his own feelings. "Any news?" he asked.

"I'm sorry, not yet. But we've got the entire force following up on leads. We have brought someone in, and he's being interrogated right now."

"Is he the one? Is there something you're not telling us?" Mrs. Walton asked anxiously.

"No, no, nothing like that."

"Well, who is he?" the husband asked. "Why him?"

Mallon knew that there would be no comfort in the answer. Kate said, "He's a convicted sex offender. This is routine. There's nothing to indicate that he has anything to do with Joey being missing."

"Oh, no," Mrs. Walton said, and collapsed onto her husband's shoulder.

There was another knock at the door, and the desk officer leaned his head in again. "Chief, there's someone here that you're going to want to—"

"We're busy right now, Nelson," Mallon all but snarled.

The officer got a strange look on his face and

opened the door fully, smiling as he stepped aside.

Mrs. Walton looked up and bolted to her feet, her mouth gaping in a soundless scream.

In the doorway stood Steve Vail. In one arm he held Joey Walton wrapped in his topcoat. His other hand was gently cradled around the back of Edward Stanton's neck.

Joey's mother rushed to him, pulling him into her arms. His father hugged them both, no longer hiding his tears. The chief sat dumbfounded, and Kate just looked at Vail, shaking her head.

Mrs. Walton asked Vail, "Was Joey . . . Is he all right?"

Vail nodded at her knowingly. "He's fine."

She tightened her arms around the child.

Vail turned the Stanton boy toward them so he could get the full impact of the reunion. Then he squatted down and looked into his eyes. "Now do you see why it's important to go back to your real parents? This mom and dad have only been separated from their son for a couple of hours, and look how they feel. Your parents have been without you for four years." The boy nodded dutifully, but Vail could see it still wasn't registering fully.

Kate came over to them and smiled. "And who is this good-looking young man?"

"This is Edward Stanton," Vail said. "He was taken in Maryland four years ago."

Kate's head snapped toward Vail. It took her a few seconds to comprehend that this boy was another kidnapping victim. "The same guy had him? How'd you find him?"

"I'll tell you later."

Kate sensed that her questions were interfering with Vail's attempt to have the Stanton boy realize that he belonged with his real parents, but, like Mrs. Walton, she couldn't help but ask about his well-being. "And he didn't . . ." She bobbed her head back and forth euphemistically so the boy wouldn't know what she was talking about.

Vail pulled Kate back away from the eleven-year-old. "Apparently not. This guy who abducted them, George Hillstrand, his wife and son died in childbirth just before he took Edward, here. He just wanted some part of his family back. As far as I can tell, Edward's been raised well. He's having a little trouble comprehending it all, figuring out where his loyalties lie, but otherwise he seems okay."

Kate watched the boy carefully. She knew that it was not unusual for long-held kidnapping victims to identify with their abductor rather than their family.

For the first time, Kate noticed that Vail's hand was wrapped in a white handkerchief and was damp with blood. "Are you all right?"

"That depends. Do you believe in sympathy dates?"

"Obviously you're fine." She looked closely at him and then back at his hand, as if putting off some argument until they could be alone.

The chief came over and asked Vail how he'd found the boys. Vail explained about the race photos and how Hillstrand's name had come up in the Maryland investigation. "Where is Hillstrand?" Mallon asked.

Vail took Kate's car keys out of his pocket and

tossed them to Mallon. "I didn't have any cuffs, so I duct-taped him and put him in the trunk."

"What happened to your hand?"

"In all the excitement, I must have cut it."

The phone rang, and Mallon picked it up, listening for a moment. "Okay, give us a few minutes." He hung up. "The media is on the way. Straighten your tie, Steve, you're about to be a hero." The chief nodded at the Stanton boy. "And wait till they hear about this young man also being safe and sound after all this time."

Kate looked at Vail and knew what he was thinking. "Tim, we appreciate it, but this is your time. Just mention that the FBI assisted in the investigation."

"Are you kidding me? I can't take credit for this."

Kate cleared her throat, signaling Vail that she was about to tell a lie. She nodded for Mallon to follow her and Vail out of the room. In the hallway she said, "Tim, I'm sorry, but I wasn't being straight with you when I said Steve wasn't with the Bureau. This is classified. You'll have to tell your people and the Waltons not to say anything about his involvement. He's been working a major municipal corruption case undercover in Chicago as a bricklayer. His name or face in the news will blow two years of hard work. Just tell the media what I told you: An undercover agent found them and is involved in an ongoing investigation. Except lie about Chicago. Since Edward was taken in Maryland, tell them it was Baltimore. That'll keep them running around in circles until this calms down. And don't be too modest—you are the one who called us."

"Kate, I may have worked applicants my whole career, but I was in the same FBI as you. Plus, I know what a terrible liar you are. I don't understand why Steve wants to duck this, but I'm too indebted to you both to question it. I'll just assume it's necessary." He gingerly shook Vail's hand, just interlocking fingertips to avoid the wound. "Whether you're an agent or not, Steve, I am most grateful." Mallon hugged Kate. Then he walked back into his office and said to the Stanton boy, "Edward, what do you say we go call your parents?"

"Yes, sir," the boy answered, his voice starting to gain some enthusiasm.

Kate unwrapped Vail's hand, revealing the grazing wound. Fortunately, the round had hit only the fleshy edge. "You're going to need some stitches."

Vail tightened the handkerchief back around his hand. "I've been here less than four hours and you've already gotten me shot."

"Me? You're the one going off on your own. *Again.* How is this my fault?"

"I don't know. Every time I get near you, something like this happens. It's like you're crime's version of Typhoid Mary."

On their way out, Vail remembered something and detoured back through the detective bureau. He picked up the note he'd left on the desk and handed it to her. "Before we have an argument, I just wanted you to know that I wasn't cutting you out. When I left here, I was cursing myself for not going with you, because your lead looked so much better."

Kate glanced at the note. "You're getting a lot better at covering your tracks."

"From your tone, apparently not good enough. Just remember who unleashed the hounds. I am a simple mason who was looking forward to free liquor and unsuspecting maidens." Vail checked the clock on the wall. "Happy New Year, Deputy Assistant Director Bannon." He kissed her lightly on the cheek, trying to determine if they were back on a date. Her response was disappointingly neutral. "Pace yourself, woman, we've got the whole night in front of us."

This was how it was with Vail, she thought. If there was a mystery in front of them, he was amazing, but once it was over, difficulties between them were inevitable. "Just because you rescued a couple of kids and got a little shot up, don't think that I'm waving you in for a landing, Vail."

When she called him "Vail," it was a good sign. She used it only when she wasn't mad. As they walked out into the parking lot, she took his arm, her touch sending electricity through him.

By the time they left the emergency room less than an hour later, dawn was coming up. Vail had taken four stitches in his hand, and the doctor had told him there shouldn't be any permanent problems.

"Well, what's your poison?" Kate asked. "I guess I owe you some sack time—on the couch. I can get you to the airport later."

"Why don't you just drop me there now."

"If you'll let me buy you breakfast first."

Then Kate noticed a familiar black Lincoln Town Car idling in the parking lot, its white-gray exhaust disappearing into the icy air. It belonged to the director of the FBI. As they approached the vehicle, the driver got out.

Kate said, "Hello, Mike. What's up?"

"The director sent me to get you."

Kate looked at Vail with a mixture of apology and apprehension.

One corner of his mouth lifted sardonically. "Ever notice how seldom the really good dates start out in the emergency room?"

The driver turned to Vail. "He sent me to get both of you."

TWO

THE BLACK TOWN CAR PULLED UP TO THE CURB IN THE 1100 block of Sixteenth Street in northwest D.C. They parked in front of an old mansion that had a tall wrought-iron fence surrounding it. "Where are we, Mike?" Kate asked the driver.

Vail pointed across the street to a large tan and gray four-story residence. "That's the old Russian embassy over there."

"They're waiting inside for you," the driver said, ignoring Kate's question and Vail's observation.

As they got out, Vail pointed at the building they were about to enter and said, "This is the old observation post where the Bureau used to monitor who came and went across the street, but then the Russians built that big compound up on Tunlaw Road, so this place was no longer necessary. Apparently they've found some new use for it."

When Kate and Vail walked up to the entrance of the huge old dwelling, an agent who was not wearing his suit coat opened one of its heavy, ten-foot-tall oak doors. Along with his sidearm, two magazine pouches were clipped to his belt. He studied both of their faces briefly and then, in a voice that was neither welcoming nor overly official, said, "The director is waiting for you upstairs."

THEY FOLLOWED A curved staircase to the second floor, and Vail took a moment to appreciate the crafts-manship of the elegant structure, which he esti-mated to be at least seventy-five years old. The staircase was constructed of Spanish black marble that was almost without any impurities to distort its ebony gloss. A large but delicate glass chandelier hung down through the helix of stairs. "Okay, I'll ask first," he said to Kate. "What's going on?"

"Not a clue," she said. "But considering that today's a holiday, the smart money is that it's not going to be good news."

"Next time *I'm* planning the date. Someplace without telephones or emergency rooms. Or FBI directors."

"Do you think if you use the word 'date' enough times, we'll actually be on one?"

"I'm hoping you'll admire me for my persever-ance."

"Isn't that the stalker's official mantra?"

On the second floor, they could hear low voices coming from a room that faced the street. They walked in, and Vail could see that it had once been an oversize bedroom but was now filled with equip-ment that looked dated. Metal tables, recording equipment, a small telescope on a long table at the window—which was covered with what he recognized as a one-way shade. A second telescope stood on a smaller table at an adjoining window, also shaded.

Aside from the director, there were five other men in the room sitting on a couch and chairs. As they entered, Vail was surprised that most of their curiosity seemed to be directed toward him. A room full of men invariably turned their attention to Kate when she entered, even if they already knew her.

Bob Lasker got to his feet and shook hands with Vail. "Steve, how's the hand?"

"It's fine."

The director nodded to one of the men, who got up and closed the door. "Good morning, Kate," Lasker said.

She looked at the faces of the other men. "Is it a good morning, sir?"

"We're about to find out. Please, both of you, have a seat. Kate, I think you know everybody here." The director then introduced the others to Vail. "Bill Langston is the assistant director in charge of the Counterintelligence Division. His deputy, John Kalix. Tony Battly, Jake Canton, and Mark Brogdon are unit and section chiefs within the division."

The director watched as Vail gave them each a snapshot evaluation. It was something Lasker wanted him to do, something that would help convince Vail to grant the request Lasker was about to make, that these men, while adequate administrators, were unqualified to do fieldwork.

The three unit and section chiefs were startlingly nondescript, reminding Vail that at FBI headquarters individuality was rewarded only with suspicion. Each of the men was overweight, as if even that shortcoming also met some sort of Bureau standard. Their suits varied little in color or quality and had become too small due to burgeoning waistlines. The sleeves on Battly's jacket were too long, covering half of his thumbs. Judging by the wear on the elbows, it had fit him that way since its purchase years before, and he'd never felt the need to have the minor tailoring done, probably because he took it off at his desk.

Brogdon's suit was equally fatigued, the pant cuffs frayed, the lapels wilted and beginning to curl up. Canton's shirt collar was too tight and had been left unbuttoned. Dusty spots dotted his tie where he had apparently scraped away food particles. The apprehensive expressions on all three faces, aside from their momentary curiosity about Vail, were those of men who were much closer to retirement than to taking on anything remotely associated with the unpredictable rigors of the street.

John Kalix, although not overweight, had a round, doughy face that was aged prematurely by a receding hairline that he made more prominent by combing over what was left of his mousy brown hair. Sitting to his boss's right, he somehow managed to mimic the assistant director's slightest movements. He wore the ageless uniform of an FBI manager: gray slacks, navy blazer, white shirt, and a striped tie that had been knotted too many times between cleanings.

On the other hand, Bill Langston, the assistant director in charge, looked like the second most important man in the room. In his mid-fifties, he was trim, even thin. He had a full head of brown hair that was going gray at the temples. His suit was moderately expensive, and he sat with his legs carefully crossed so as to not wrinkle the sharp creases along the front of his trousers. His posture was unusually erect, as though he were waiting for an "unexpected" photo. The expression on his face, somehow inappropriate for the moment, was one of patrician stoicism. Vail guessed that it was an effort on his part not to be easily read.

"Steve, I never did get a chance, face-to-face, to thank you for what you did during the Pentad investigation in L.A.," the director said. "I've told everyone here about your involvement in the case."

Waving his hand in the direction of Kate, Vail said, "As a result you offered this one a promotion—some thank-you."

Lasker smiled. "Speaking of which, nice work last night on those abductions, Kate. We're getting a ton of good press for a change."

"Since your driver knew to pick us up at the emergency room, I assume you talked to the chief in Reston. To be honest, sir, the only thing I had to do with finding those boys was driving Steve there."

"Looks like you were going somewhere nice before you got sidetracked."

Vail spoke first so that Kate wouldn't have to be embarrassed by trying to explain the circumstances of their failed date. "The Irish ambassador's reception. Just as well. I don't speak the language."

The director laughed. "You and Washington's elite in the same room, Steve? That would have been worth the price of admission."

"You might have been disappointed. I was under strict orders to keep my shirt on and not arm-wrestle anyone for beer." Vail cocked his head to one side to let the director know that he was becoming suspicious of the small talk. "But then I doubt we're here to catch up on my lack of social breeding."

"Sorry," Lasker said. The single word seemed genuine. "We've got a major problem. There's no way to make this sound like it's not hyperbole, but it is legitimately a matter of national security. The people in this room are the only ones who know what I'm going to tell you."

"Classified, I got it."

"I've been through your old personnel file again, so I know you've been trained in counterintelligence." Because of a master's degree in Soviet history, Vail had originally been hired to work the Russians. Out of training school, he'd been sent to Detroit to work general criminal cases in order to develop broader investigative skills, but he was frequently sent back to Quantico for in-service training. That's how he knew about the old embassy across the street and the building they were now in. "Other than the technology, not much has changed. It's still pretty much cloak-and-dagger. Actually, more cloaks than daggers. Have you followed any of the recent cases?"

"I've always been interested in anything American-Russian, so I read a lot of what's published."

"Good, then we won't have to waste time explaining every nuance of how all this works. Bill, can you fill him in?"

The assistant director stood up, went over to a laptop computer, and tapped a key. The wall above the fireplace, which was being used as a makeshift screen, lit up. A photograph of grainy surveillance quality appeared, showing a man with the flat, pale features of an Eastern European, his sideburns and mustache a little too bushy to be stylish in the United States. "A month ago this individual contacted our Washington Field Office and requested a meeting. He was guarded in the information he supplied but said that he was an intelligence officer with the Russian embassy here in Washington. He would not identify himself by name but instead used the code name Calculus. At this meeting, to qualify himself as legitimate, he turned over five classified documents. When we asked him what he wanted from us, he said he had a list of Americans, some employed by the government and some by corporations with defense contracts, who were supplying information to the SVR, which if you've been keeping up, know is the new KGB. He wouldn't say how many were on the list or where they worked. However, one of the individuals, he was certain, worked in the U.S. intelligence community. He didn't know which agency."

"The documents he turned over—how critical was the information?" Vail asked.

"Nothing earth-shattering, but enough to convince us that he could have access to what he claimed. Why do you ask that?"

"Just curious."

Kate watched Vail carefully. She detected a note of discovery in his voice.

"I assume he wants money," Vail said.

"Why else would someone betray Mother Russia and risk the executioner?" Langston said. "The way he set it up was quite clever. He would give us, in his words, the 'smallest fish first, the largest, last,' which we assume is the intelligence agent. Once we identified the first one, we were to wire-transfer a quarter of a million dollars to a Chicago bank, for which he provided an account number. He said it's a large bank and that the account, which was opened by one of his relatives who works there, is in a dummy name. He warned that if the Bureau tried to find out who it was or trace the funds, the relative would be alerted and all contact with us would be severed, because if he couldn't trust us, he was as good as dead. Once the relative notified him that the money had been deposited, we would get the next name. He wanted a quarter of a million for each of them and a half million for the last one, because according to him it's a *highly placed* intelligence agent."

"Did he say how quickly after payment you would get the next name?"

"In fact, he made that quite clear. We would get it, in his words, 'immediately if not sooner,' because he felt the longer this dragged out, the better the chances of his being exposed. He said the SVR had been given strict orders by Moscow that it must never become public knowledge that the Russians were spying on the United States again. Although their agents are extremely cautious to start with, apparently that directive has made them completely paranoid. Even the faintest hint of disloyalty launches an all-out probe."

Vail said, "So he gives you a name, you arrest that person, and then wire a quarter of a million dollars to the Chicago account. Once it's deposited, you get the next name, and so on until the intelligence agent is caught, and then you send a half million."

"Right."

"Does that mean he's given you the first name?"

"More or less," the assistant director said.

"As far as spycraft goes," Vail said to the director, "this sounds pretty paint-by-the-numbers. Why am I here?"

"A couple of reasons," Langston said. "Two days ago we got a short, cryptic text message from him. He has been recalled to Moscow unexpectedly."

"Uh-oh," Vail said.

"What?" Kate asked.

"When someone is suspected of spying, the Russians find some routine excuse to get them back to Moscow. Once there, they're interrogated, for months if necessary. Should they confess or if the SVR develops any proof, the suspected individual is usually executed for treason. And since it's not something the Russians are likely to make public, you'd never know," Vail said.

Langston continued, "Since the first letter, we've been trying to identify Calculus. And now we think we know who he is. The CIA has a fairly high-level source in the Russian embassy. In a rare act of cooperation, they've identified an individual for us. If they've given us the right name, he's an electrical engineer by training and is extremely cautious, even obsessive, which in the spy business is a good thing. His job is what we call a technical agent. He's sent all over the United States to their safe houses to wire them for sound and video and record meetings in case any of their double agents should get cold feet. Then they could be threatened with exposure, a foolproof way of keeping an asset's attention. The rest of it we're guessing at. We think, after meetings between American sources and their Russian handlers, he would collect the recordings and store them at the embassy. We think that with his financial future in mind, he started making a list of their identities. Maybe even keeping copies of the documents they turned over or other information we could use as corroborating evidence."

Vail said, "You got to love a communist who appreciates capitalism more than we do."

"Exactly."

Vail asked, "Well, let me ask you—hopefully for the last time—why me?"

"The only ones who know about this are the people in this room. If we gave this to any of our agents, I guarantee it would leak out. Your discretion has been established more than once. You have a certain reputation for getting things done despite obstacles that our agents would find . . . well, procedurally insurmountable."

Vail laughed. "You mean none of you want to get caught."

The director said, "The rest of us here are not exactly street-ready, and this has the potential to get *challenging*. The men in this room haven't been out there in decades." Lasker glanced around to see if anyone objected. "Sorry, guys."

Vail glanced at Kate and then back at the director. "When you offered me this kind of arrangement before, I said no."

The director pursed his lips. "That was because I thought your not being an agent was a waste of talent and I was hoping you'd eventually realize it. When you were vehement, I accepted it. But this is different. This is vital."

Vail got up and walked over to the window. He raised the shade and stared at the old Russian embassy across the street. "Funny, five years ago I thought this was exactly what I'd be doing right now. Instead I'm a bricklayer." He turned back and looked at the men. "While you may find that ironic, I find it unjust."

"Steve, we have to assume that Calculus is being interrogated in Moscow right now. If the Russians break him, there will be no list and all those spies will go on selling our secrets."

"I'm sorry. I'm going home."

Everyone in the room was silent. Finally the director said, "Could you come with me for a minute? There's something you need to see."

Vail followed him downstairs and then through a series of small, unfurnished rooms.

Once Lasker was satisfied they were completely out of earshot of the others, he said, "Did Kate tell you what happened to her just before Thanksgiving?"

"No."

"She almost died."

"*What?*"

"She left her car running at her place as well as the door to the garage open. She'd been drinking. Wound up in the hospital for a couple of days."

"You think it was a suicide attempt?" Vail's voice was accusatory.

"No, I don't. But it was a couple of days after she'd gone to see you in Chicago, which OPR tells me did not go well."

"Kate's way too strong for anything like that. And as up and down as we've been, I've never seen her depressed for a second."

"I couldn't agree more."

"She dumped me. I'm the one who's supposed to be suicidal."

"I thought you guys made up. Isn't that why you're here?"

"That was a lie. She didn't know I was coming. I was trying to patch things up. She was driving me back to the airport when she got the kidnapping call."

"Like I said, I know it wasn't a suicide attempt, but I can't call off the OPR investigation just because I think so. I'm sure you can remember how petty people can be in this organization when it comes to someone else's problems. When somebody is as successful as Kate is, they want to believe it. She's got people looking at her like she's a time bomb. I want her to work with you on this Calculus thing. If you two did half the job you did in L.A., all that petty whispering would come to a screeching halt."

Vail laughed. "Are you blowing this out of proportion to hook me?"

"When you and she walked into that room upstairs, did you notice that none of those men would look at her? When's the last time you saw that happen?"

Vail took a moment to consider what Lasker had said. "I'd be a fool to say yes to this." There was something in Vail's tone that told the director that was exactly what he was about to do. "Fortunately for you, it's not exactly construction weather in Chicago."

Lasker clapped him on the shoulder. "Thanks."

When they walked back into the upstairs room, the director said, "Steve's decided to give us a hand, and Kate will work with him."

Kate's eyes locked onto Vail. She had heard the surety in his tone when he'd said no to the director. She'd never seen him change his mind once it was so firmly set.

Vail looked back at her. "However, this time, if you're going to saddle me with Deputy Assistant Director Bannon, she has to understand that I am working *with* and not *for* her?"

Kate took a moment to recover and then said, "Yes, those were the two big disruptions in L.A., me giving orders and you following them."

The director looked slightly distracted by what he was about to say, missing the humor in Kate's response. "I know how you feel about answering to anyone, Steve, but because this is so potentially explosive, I'm going to need you or Kate to report to Bill at least once a day so he can keep me advised."

"Define 'report to,'" Vail said.

"This is extremely complicated, so I need everyone to work together. Whatever other intelligence agency might be involved, add in the Russians and our own State Department and it's going to be a diplomatic high-wire act. The potential for disaster is incalculable. You have to keep Bill advised."

"Is that actually what you want us to do, or are you giving me one of those orders that when you're called in front of some congressional subcommittee, you can say I disregarded your instructions? If it's the second, I have no problem with it."

"I'm sorry, Steve, I need you to report daily. I wouldn't be much of a director if I didn't keep a very close eye on this one."

Vail knew that because of Kate he had no choice. "You do realize how this is going to end."

"I'm hoping it doesn't."

"Which means you can see exactly how it's going to end," Vail said. "Kate, I've got to tell you that this is the worst date I've ever been on." She just shook her head. "Guys, consider yourselves warned: This is not who I am, but I'll do what I can."

"Thank you," Lasker said.

Vail turned to the assistant director. "Bill, I don't know you at all. What I'm about to say is based on my personal history with Bureau bosses. If it doesn't apply, ignore it."

His face expressionless, Langston said, "Go ahead."

"If you try to obstruct me simply because of your ego, I'll be on the first available flight to Chicago, and I'm going to guess that won't make the director happy." Langston still showed no reaction. Vail turned to the others. "Okay, then, does anybody have any ideas where to start?"

The deputy assistant director, John Kalix, said, "The second time we met with Calculus, we had finished analyzing the documents that he had turned over to us and knew that he was legit, so we gave him a special phone. He was supposed to use it only to contact us. It's a miniaturized satellite phone, very ordinary-looking. That's all we told him about it. It had other capabilities, one of which was to constantly track his position, even when it was supposedly turned off. He used it only once, to text us about being recalled to Moscow. Six words, that's all. That was the last time we heard from him." Kalix got up and tapped the computer keyboard. A photograph of the message appeared.

To Moscow unexpectedly. Find CDP now!

"We're guessing 'CDP' are the initials of the first person on his list," Kalix continued. "We've checked them through every available database, most of which don't have middle initials, and have no clue who it is. Not everyone lists a middle initial. There could be hundreds, even thousands of them across the country. It's not much to go on. The only other thing we have is where he traveled. It's all documented in the dark blue file on the table there."

Vail took a moment to process what he'd been told and then looked over at the folder and nodded. "And where is the phone now?"

"As soon as that message was sent, we could no longer determine where it was. Somehow the GPS must have been disabled."

"The last location?"

"Inside the Russian embassy."

"That doesn't sound promising. Anything else that might help us?"

"That's it. Like I said, it's not much to go on."

The director stood up. "Thank you, guys." The men understood that the meeting was at an end and they were to leave.

After everyone filed out, the director closed the door behind them. "Steve, you two should probably work out of here. It's secure, and there's some equipment you might be able to use. The computers are current and have complete Bureau access. The building is alarmed, and there's a stocked kitchen, a shower, and some cots for sleeping. The briefcase on the table is for you. Gun, credentials, credit card, cell phone are all inside. Parked out front is a blue Chevy sedan. The keys are in the case, too." He took out a blank business-size card and wrote down a number on it. "If you need anything else—*anything*—call this number."

Vail said, "Any objections if I move in here?"

The director glanced at Kate. "If that's what you prefer, sure."

"It'll eliminate travel time from the hotel," Vail said, and Kate understood that he had offered the reason so she wouldn't be embarrassed at whatever way the director interpreted their relationship.

"And I'm only about fifteen minutes away," she said.

Vail said, "If we round up any of these people, aren't you afraid it'll point the Russians in Calculus's direction? If they're not already onto him."

"We do have an obligation to try to protect him as best we can, but we have a greater duty to protect this country. Actually, we have discussed our options for keeping this quiet as long as possible. Through legal and bureaucratic foot-dragging, we figure the whole thing could be kept quiet for about ten days. So if you do bring someone in, that ten-day clock will start ticking. After that, I'm afraid Calculus's anonymity could become tenuous."

Kate said, "Ten days isn't much time to get from A to Z. Especially since we're not sure where A is or how many letters there are in the alphabet."

"No, it's not. And to compound the problem, we don't know if we'll get any more information from Calculus. Steve, you have no idea how much I appreciate this. Between keeping everything secret and the idea of a bunch of traitors running around Washington, it was an impossible challenge. But now we have you. I'm sorry about handcuffing you with reporting daily, but this is a completely different situation from Los Angeles. If you have any problems, you've got my number."

"'Abandon all hope, ye who enter here!'"

The director smiled. "Dante, right?"

"Rather than who wrote it, it's more important to know where it was posted."

"Which is?"

"It was the inscription at the gate to hell."

THREE

AFTER KATE HAD WALKED THE DIRECTOR OUT, SHE CAME back upstairs. "Thank you for doing this. And for protecting my reputation with the director."

"Oh, how I wish your reputation actually needed protection."

"Me, too, Vail."

He stared at her for a few seconds and then went back to the window, again staring at the old embassy across the street.

She said, "What exactly did the director show you downstairs that changed your mind?"

"A large sum of money."

"*Vail.*"

"Okay, he played 'America the Beautiful.'" She scowled at him. "Metaphorically. He knew that if he got me out of that room, and away from all that *management*, my decision would be less knee-jerk. For being the big boss, he gets a pretty good read on people."

Kate studied Vail's face for a few seconds, looking for deception. "I wish I could get a good read on you."

"That's the other reason we have trouble getting along. You think I always have a secret agenda."

"Where would anyone get an idea like that?"

"See, that's why I think there's hope for us. If our relationship didn't have a healthy foundation, you would've taken a cheap shot right there."

Kate smiled and shook her head. "Where do you want to start?"

"It's been thirty-six hours since either of us slept. I'm going to get a few hours' sleep. I suggest you do the same."

"I need to change, too. I'll take the car back to my place. I'll bring up your suitcase when I come back."

"I'm starving. Let's see how we're set for food first."

As he started for the kitchen, she said, "This time I need to be on the inside of the investigation, Steve."

"Okay, but just remember it comes with a lot of liability."

"Have I ever denied you when you wanted to commit a felony?"

"I said you're in, Deputy Assistant Director Bannon."

"Then explain your question about the classified documents Calculus gave up. What was that about? And don't give me that 'curious' stuff. I've seen that look before."

"Well, isn't this getting off to a familiar start?" Vail said, laughing for a moment. "Sometimes in the spy business, your opponents will run a game on you. They'll salt the mines with borderline information to convince you that they're on your side. It's just something to be wary of. And if they're good, they can wind up getting more information from you than you get from them."

She stared at him for a few seconds. "That *sounds* like a reasonable explanation, but it always does— and then suddenly I'm being shot at."

"There are worse things than being shot at."

"Like . . . ?"

"Living a life where you're never shot at." He went into the kitchen and yelled out to her. "These are spies. They don't shoot at people. But I'd be careful what I ate." The refrigerator was stocked with food, including a carton of eggs. He took them out and checked the date. "These eggs are fresh. How about I make some breakfast?"

"I assume that you have no desire to poison me."

"Sure, we'll say that."

"Do you want me to do that?" she asked.

"I'm just going to scramble some eggs. Why don't you have a look through those files they left us."

Ten minutes later he walked out with two plates loaded with eggs and toast balanced on top. She looked at the plate he set in front of her. "Make enough?"

"With you I never know when I'm going to get to eat again." He picked up his fork. "Anything in the files?"

She took a bite of toast and pulled a photograph from the back of the file. "Here's that shot of Calculus's message."

She watched him carefully as he laid it on the table next to his plate and studied it while he continued to eat.

To Moscow unexpectedly. Find CDP now!

Finally she said, "Do you think CDP is our 'little fish'?"

Vail continued to eat, staring at the message. "It has to be. He uses only three words to notify us of his possible impending death: 'To Moscow unexpectedly.' Someone that economical wouldn't waste the last three words on something meaningless. He used exactly the same number of words to indicate that they're as important as the first three."

"Why would he care whether we found the spies if he knew he was going to be taken back there and tortured, and probably worse?"

Again Vail was lost in thought. She took a mouthful of eggs and watched him as he ate absentmindedly. Finally he said, "This is good. Very, very good."

"The eggs?"

"Your question about him caring. It could be the key to unlocking this. He shouldn't care. Yet he sent us the first mole's initials. Why?"

"Maybe he figured since he was being sent back to Moscow, he'd give us the first name hoping we'd send the money to the Chicago bank and it would get to his family or whoever."

"That's a possibility. Here's another one: What if he planned for this contingency? He knew that if the Russians get it out of him about the list and recover what he's hidden for us, they'll have all they need to convict him of treason and execute him. But if he can get us to whatever evidence he left for us, before the Russians can recover it, they won't be able to prove a thing. Maybe he's in Moscow right now enduring torture to give us whatever head start he can."

"It's urgent, I get it. But first we have to find this CPD. How do we do that? Like Kalix said, there's got to be a lot of people with those initials."

"Another good question. Unfortunately, one that is going to require a little sleep to answer. I hate to waste the time sleeping, but it'll be a good investment." Vail picked up his plate and asked her, "Are you done?"

"Yes, thanks."

"Can you be back here in four hours?"

"Seeing how the alternative is to let you go wandering off with a new set of credentials and a gun, and then having to answer to the director, I guess I'll have to."

ALMOST TO THE minute, four hours after leaving him, Kate pulled up in front of the old Bureau observation post. It was midafternoon, but the temperature was still near freezing. She took his suitcase out of the trunk and carried it upstairs. He was in the room where the meeting with the director had taken place. He had shaved and showered and was reading one of the files that had been provided.

"It didn't take you long to get back at it. Anything in there?" she asked.

"There is one interesting thing. The cell phone they gave Calculus, it tracked him twenty-four hours a day. We have detailed coordinate charts telling us where he went and when."

"Nothing else?"

"Not yet, but I'm already getting the feeling I'm missing something." He stood up and went over to a computer that was on. "Take a look at this. You've probably seen it before."

She peered over his shoulder. "Sure, that's a spy satellite we have access to. How'd you know about it?"

"I kept reading in the file about transverse tracking. When I turned on the computer, I saw the icon on the desktop." She sat down in a chair next to him. "I looked through those cell-phone GPS logs. I think they're important."

"Important how?"

"Take a look at his message again." He handed her the file. "How do the last three words differ from the first three?"

To Moscow unexpectedly. Find CDP now!

"The exclamation point?"

"And . . . ?"

She looked for a few seconds and then shook her head in frustration. "I don't know, what?"

"Look at my hand," he said, holding it with the fingers spread as wide as possible. "Now look at the message again."

She did and then said, "It looks like there's an extra space between the 'CPD' and the word 'now.'" She thought about it a little longer. "I still don't get it."

"I made some coffee. Would you mind getting me a cup?" His voice was more instructional than demanding.

Her face shortened into a knot of confusion. "Oooo-kay." She went into the kitchen and started pouring coffee into a mug. "Black?" she called out to him. Before he could answer, she yelled, "The last sentence contains a message within a message!" Forgetting the coffee, she hurried back into the room. "If he didn't mean anything by it, the exclamation point would been after 'To Moscow unexpectedly,' to emphasize the danger he was in. But using it with 'now' and isolating it with an extra space indicates that there are two messages within those last three words: Find CDP and an instruction to do it *now*, at that exact moment." She grinned, realizing that Vail had sent her to get coffee so she would stop staring at the forest and be able to isolate one of the trees.

"And what are we in possession of that can quantify 'now'?" he asked.

This time Kate let her mind go blank before trying to figure out the answer. "The exact time he sent the message."

Vail said, "And since we have his exact longitude and latitude when he sent it, he might have been giving us a clue to who CDP is."

"But he would have to know that the phone we gave him was capable of tracking his movements."

"First of all, he's an engineer, an engineer in the spy business—don't you think he would assume that? Why would we give him just an ordinary satellite phone? Plus, the phone was turned on. He'd have to know we could track him then." Vail handed her the file; it was opened to the GPS charts. He turned back to the computer and the satellite imaging. "The call was made on December twenty-ninth at 4:18 P.M. Give me the coordinates listed for that time."

As she read them, Vail maneuvered the mouse over a map of the United States until the digits in the small display windows were the same as those she had given him. He locked them in and then used the on-screen control to zoom down to the location, which could be seen with incredible detail, close enough to capture the address from an adjoining map on the screen. "It's some sort of business. There are dozens of cars in that front parking lot alone."

"Here, let me," Kate said.

Vail got up, and Kate sat down at the computer. She went to a different search engine and typed in the address. A corporate profile popped up on the screen. "Alliant Industries in Calverton, Virginia." She clicked on another icon and was shifted into Bureau indices and searched the name. "There it is, Alliant Industries. They're in our files because we've done quite a few background investigations on their employees for security clearances. Evidently they have some defense contracts."

"Can you pull up the list of names that we've investigated?"

"Hold on." She typed some more, waited until the results came up on the screen, and then started scrolling through the alphabetical list. "Believe it or not, there are two with the first initial C and last initial P: Claudia Prinzon and Charles Pollock. Let me see if I can find middle initials."

She started to open the background report on the woman when Vail said, "Don't bother. It's Pollock."

"How do you know?"

"Pollock is a North Atlantic food fish. *Our* little fish."

She shook her head and laughed. "This isn't going to make the Counterintelligence Division very happy."

"Why not?"

"How do you think they're going to take it when I tell them that you found the first mole in less than four hours, not counting sleeping, showering, and shaving time? I know you're not trying to make them look like idiots, but . . ."

Vail laughed. "Maybe that's why I keep getting fired."

"*Maybe?*"

"Then let's not tell them."

"You know that's not possible. Now that we know who Pollock is, we'll have to start twenty-four-hour surveillance and get up on his phones and computer ASAP. And eventually search warrants. Are you going to do all that by yourself?"

"Okay, we'll wait a couple of days before we tell anyone. That way it'll look like it was a lot more difficult."

"Hi, I'm Kate Bannon. We met last year. Apparently you don't remember me because you're trying to run the same scam on me as you did then. You're still trying to end-run everyone. And in case you're counting, 'everyone' includes *me*."

"It doesn't include you. Wherever this takes me, it takes us. It's just that the more *they* get involved, the farther away the answer always seems to get. They're like moths."

"Moths?"

"They keep flying into the light simply because it's the brightest thing in front of them, even though they're slowly beating themselves—and any chance to solve this case—to death."

"Give it up, Vail. At some point even you are going to need Bureau help."

"As clever as Calculus has been with this, maybe he's hidden evidence somewhere out there, and if we're equally smart, we can find it without wasting all that time and manpower."

"You're not worried about wasting Bureau resources. If anything, you like burning them. You're just dreaming up excuses to cover up whatever you really have in mind."

"Come on, Kate, we're ahead of schedule. Let's poke around a little and see what we can find. It's New Year's Day. There are hangovers to nurse, there's football to watch, resolutions to fake. Nobody wants to hear from us."

"Define 'poke around,'" she said, with even more caution than usual.

"It's a holiday. We have a car, a credit card, and all of Calculus's locations for the last two weeks he was here. Let's take a ride and see if he left anything else to find."

She shook her head with mild self-contempt. "You make it sound so simple, so right, and even though I know it's neither, I'm going to go along with it."

"Am I a good time or what?"

"I'll admit that it always seems like it's going to be a good time, but it usually turns out to be 'or what.'"

FOUR

WHEN THEY GOT TO THE CAR, VAIL SAID, "YOU KNOW YOUR way around here a lot better than I do, so why don't I drive?"

While he drove, Kate made a list of everywhere Calculus had traveled on the day he sent his last message. "Okay, but you've got your work cut out for you. He drove over two hundred miles outside the D.C. area."

"In one day? That seems like a lot, but then maybe he wanted us to notice."

"Where do we start?"

"How about at his clue, Alliant Industries in Calverton."

She found the address in her notes and entered it into the GPS unit on the dashboard. "Do you have any idea what we're looking for?"

"What we always look for, those wonderful little failed attempts to hide the truth—anomalies."

When he offered no further specifics, she said, "These anomalies, any idea what form they might take?"

"Not a clue. I was just hoping that being philosophically vague would impress you into quiet contemplation."

"I'm a little surprised that you're still trying to impress me."

Vail couldn't tell whether the comment was meant to be sarcastic or whether she was offering some sort of truce. "Just because I can be an idiot, that doesn't mean you're not worth impressing. Who knows, maybe I could change."

"If you did, you'd probably bore me to death."

"Do you know why male moths fly so close to the flame of a candle?" he said mischievously, knowing she would object to any more moth references.

"Oh, so you *are* trying to bore me to death."

"The flame gives off a vibrational frequency similar to the female moth's pheromone. The male moth is powerfully attracted to it, even though it's extremely dangerous."

"In other words, even setting yourselves on fire won't deter you guys."

"I'm here, driving into who-knows-what, if that answers your question."

"You want me to tell you what I think? I think you're bored right now and hoping you'll drive into exactly 'who-knows-what.'"

For the next three hours, they traced the route the Russian engineer had taken through Virginia, stopping where he had, according to the Bureau charts. Each time, Kate would get out and take photos of everything in sight, making notes about the corresponding locations. Halfway back, they found a diner and he pulled in.

Inside, they sat in a booth, and after the waitress had taken their orders, Kate asked, "Well, any anomalies?"

"Not yet. But I want to spend some time with everything back at the off-site. Kind of let it all percolate a little."

"It sounds like you want to be alone."

"You're welcome to stick around, but a lot of it is going to be just busywork—printing out photos, matching them with the maps and timelines. I'm not sure you want to spend your evening like that. By morning I'll have everything a little more organized and we'll be able to figure out what our next move is."

"So in the morning there won't be an article in the paper about you breaking into the Russian embassy or involved in a shooting somewhere?"

"I can't make any promises about the embassy, but you have my word I'll never get involved in a shoot-out without you."

"In that case I'm going to go home, get out a pad of paper and a pencil, and retrace my life as far back as I have to, to try to determine what seemingly innocuous, small turn in my life caused it to intersect with yours."

"You know, there's an old Chinese proverb that says if you try to learn the source of your good fortune, you will destroy it."

"What I know is that if the Chinese actually do believe that, it's because they've never met you."

THE NEXT MORNING Kate let herself into the off-site and could smell coffee brewing as she started up the stairs. She found that Vail had pushed all the furniture away from the longest wall in the room and had taped up all the photos from the day before. Below them were the time-place maps that had guided their trip.

"Did you get any sleep?" she asked.

"Enough. Did you eat?"

"I just need some coffee."

"I think it's done. Grab a cup and let's go."

"Where to?"

"Pollock's bank in Calverton."

"For?"

"I want to look at his account records."

"For?"

Vail pointed at the wall. "Remember where we stopped in Denton?"

"I'd have to look at the photos." She stepped closer to the wall.

"It's a small intersection. There's nothing there but that house."

She looked at the photo of a small, white wood-frame structure pinned to the wall.

"According to the map, Calculus was there for about two and a half hours at night. None of his other stops were anywhere near that long."

"Wait a minute. How do you know which bank is Pollock's?"

"It's in his security-clearance investigation."

"And how do his bank records tie in?"

"If he visited his bank within twenty-four hours of Calculus's stop at that house, then I think there's a good chance that Pollock made an exchange with his handler there and Calculus recorded it. So the next day Pollock would have to deposit the money, unless he keeps it under his mattress."

"Does that mean we're going to let the assistant director—or anyone else—in on this?"

"Not yet."

"Then how are you going to get bank records without some sort of court order?"

"With this." Vail held up a standard information-release form filled out and signed by Pollock.

"Where did you get that?"

"We did a background investigation on him, didn't we? And isn't part of that process for him to sign information releases?"

"How did you get into his file?"

"You let me watch your hands when you logged into the Bureau database yesterday, so I thought you were giving me your password."

She just shook her head. "But Pollock's background was almost five years ago. Those forms would be out of date." She looked closer. "It's dated a week ago."

"A little Wite-Out, a copying machine, and everything's up to date in Kansas City."

"You'll have to excuse me if I seem a little slow. I've been back here for six months, you know, following the law and stuff. Throws a girl off."

AN HOUR LATER Vail pulled up to the Denton Savings and Loan. "Since you're apparently too chicken to violate both the national banking laws and the Privacy Act, you can wait here." He got out and walked inside.

In another twenty minutes, he came out, and Kate said, "Well?"

"The morning after Calculus's stop at the little white house, Pollock deposited eighty-nine hundred dollars into his checking account."

"Eighty-nine hundred is a nice number. It keeps it under ten thousand so the IRS isn't notified, but not as noticeable as ninety-nine hundred, which is a bigger flag than if he had deposited the entire ten thousand."

Vail started the car and pulled out. "I think I know what that house is now."

"What?"

"For Calculus to be there and record the exchange, it has to be a Russian safe house. Maybe he left something there for us."

"So now we're going to Langston with this, right?" And then, pretending to be talking to herself, she said, "Oh, Kate, you are cute but so naïve. That's Steve Vail sitting next to you, and you're asking him about going to the AD?"

Vail laughed. "If you were the assistant director in charge of counterterrorism, what would you do?" When she didn't say anything, he said, "Come on, Kate, that was almost your job. What do you do now?"

"I'd probably black-bag it."

"And how long would that take?"

"To line up all the techs and the lock guys, do the site work, I suppose a couple of days."

"Minimum. We don't have a couple of days. The Russians have a big advantage over us—torture."

Vail turned left, and she realized he wasn't heading back to Washington. "Please tell me you're not going to break into a Russian safe house."

"You're the one who demanded to be *inside the investigation* this time. Now come the liabilities that you were warned about. You can't have it both ways."

"Here's four words I'm going to assume you've heard before: *You can't do that.* It belongs to the Russians."

"First of all, the correct pronoun is 'we.' And I can foresee only one possible problem. I noticed in the photo you took that there's an alarm-company warning sticker in the front window."

"That's why we need our tech and lock people to get inside."

"Who do you suppose was the last person out of the house that night?"

"If he was doing the technical stuff, I suppose Calculus?"

"If he left evidence for us in there, do you think he would have set the alarm?"

Kate let her head fall to her chest as if surrendering all hope. "You know, it's being exposed to guys like you that makes online dating seem so promising. The only thing a girl has to worry about there is the occasional serial killer."

FIVE

KATE LISTENED TO VAIL'S SHALLOW BREATHING AND FOUND it remarkable that he could sleep anywhere, and apparently under any circumstances. They had been watching the suspected safe house for a couple of hours, waiting for dark, and Vail, after giving her a nod that he was going to do so, had drifted off. She wondered how much sleep he'd actually had in the past two days. For the last half year, she had been back in Washington, away from him. Back to the daily dictates of organization and rules. Beyond all else, rules. So many, in fact, that following every one of them left not the slightest opportunity to get anything else done. But Vail was an outsider, someone who couldn't exist in such an inertial state. He was about to commit a burglary that carried with it the potential of international consequences. It scared the hell out of her. She looked over at him sleeping and wondered why she couldn't wait to be part of it.

As if sensing that the sun had finally set, Vail opened his eyes. He looked at the small house and said, "No lights. So far so good."

"What if someone from the embassy came back

out here and reset the alarm? If it was turned off in the first place?"

"Then I would assume we'll hear some sort of loud noise or see flashing lights. There's only one way to find out."

"Did it ever occur to you that the Russians might have some sort of sensor that goes right into the embassy and isn't connected to this alarm system?"

"That's more than an hour away."

"They could call the local police."

"We're FBI agents. We saw someone breaking in and went in after them. They must have heard us and gone out the back."

"I don't know how I could ever question you. Apparently this is another foolproof plan. I'm psyched. Dibs on the crowbar."

"That's what I like to see, Kate, some genuine enthusiasm." Vail glanced at her feet. "I guess I should have told you to wear more sensible shoes." He manipulated the map on the dashboard GPS to search the surrounding areas.

"Sensible shoes? At this moment my footwear choice is what you think may not have been well thought out?"

He pointed to the GPS screen. "I want to go through the woods behind the place and get in through a rear window or door."

She reached over and removed the keys from the ignition. "Fortunately, I have my gym clothes in the trunk." She got out and retrieved her running shoes.

As she put them on, Vail drove past the house and, then a quarter of a mile farther, turned onto a dirt road. A hundred yards later, he found a place on the shoulder wide enough to pull over and park. After taking a last look at the map on the screen, he asked, "Ready?"

"Let's burgle."

Grabbing a flashlight from the glove compartment, Vail led the way through the woods, which although heavily treed had little underbrush to navigate through. Ten minutes later they stood at the edge of a tree line looking at the back of the house. It was completely dark. The rear of the structure had no doors, but there were three identical windows. "Go knock on the door."

"Of a Russian safe house. Shouldn't I have a stack of Girl Scout cookies or be wearing a Brownie uniform?"

"This is no time for sexual fantasies. Tell them your car broke down and you need to call the auto club."

"And why would someone as together as I am—discounting my shoes—not have a cell phone?" she asked. "Is that fantasy about me or Thin Mints?"

"Tell them it's dead. You know, act like a ditz."

"There are some subtle rewards to working with you, but I think my favorite part is the Taliban-level degradation."

"I told you, save the dirty talk for later."

Kate walked to the side door and knocked. When there was no answer, she pounded her fist on it loudly, glancing back at Vail. After a minute he stepped out of the cover of the trees and waved at her to come to the rear of the house. "Start trying all the windows. If he was going to leave the alarm off, maybe he left us a way in."

The second window Kate tried slid open. "Over here."

Vail came to her and lifted himself through the window. "Hold on while I look around." She watched anxiously as the beam of his flashlight swept the room and then disappeared. When he came back, he offered her his hand. "All clear."

Once inside, Kate asked, "What are we looking for?"

"Anything locked. Doors, cabinets, anything where Calculus could have secured whatever he left."

"If he left anything. If we're burglarizing the right place."

Vail walked over to a window shade that was pulled down. He put his hand behind it and then stepped to the side so Kate could see. "One-way shades, just like at the observation post. We're in the right place."

"Then since we have only one flashlight, how about we pull all the shades down and turn on some lights?"

Vail flashed the beam around the room, trying to determine what kind of lighting the house was equipped with and if it could be seen from outside. He turned his flashlight up to the ceiling, examining the fixtures.

"What kind of bulbs are those?" Kate asked.

"Good question." He pulled over a table and got up on it. He unscrewed the bulb. It was heavy and appeared to be filled with something black. He turned it upside down and felt the granules inside shift. He screwed it back in carefully.

When he got down, Kate said, "What is it?"

"I can't be sure, but I think they were filled with gunpowder and then reassembled."

"Gunpowder?"

"If you turn on the light switch, the electricity going through the element will set them off."

"Why would they do that?"

"My guess is that Calculus did it."

"Why?"

"I'm not sure. For now just stay close to me."

Kate and Vail moved from room to room, and he scanned each section of the ceiling with his flashlight. "The Russians spent some money upgrading this house." He pointed with the beam of the flashlight. "See, they've got a sprinkler-system head in every room. Probably because their embassy is so far away. They didn't want someone to be able to come in here and burn it down."

"Like an 'accidental' fire started by a rival agency?"

"Pretty silly, huh? Can you imagine being that paranoid?" Vail walked along a short hallway into a room that looked like it was furnished and set up for meetings. He examined one wall closely, slowly sweeping his light across it. "There," he said. "Do you see it?"

Kate stepped closer. "A pinhole camera."

Vail patted the wall the camera was embedded in. "Did you notice how thick this wall is?"

"No."

He led the way back into the room on the other side, and Kate said, "Now I see what you mean. It's got to be four feet wide."

Vail started checking the narrow panels that covered it. He tapped along the wall, looking for an access point. Using both hands, he pushed against each panel. The third one clicked open an inch or so. Behind it was a four-by-six-foot room that had been soundproofed. On a shelf were a series of audio and video recorders.

He could now see the pinhole camera attached to the interior of the wall, a lead running to a video recorder and then to a small monitor, so that the asset being paid off could be carefully watched and recorded as the event was occurring.

On the sidewall was a circuit-breaker box for the entire house. Vail guessed that it had existed before they built the narrow room around it. He turned on the DVD recorder and pressed the Eject button, but the carousel was empty. On top of the monitor was a plastic kitchen bowl that seemed out of place. Inside it was a sealed paper packet. Directly above it was another sprinkler head, presumably to protect the equipment should anything happen. Instead of taking the packet out, Vail picked up the bowl and examined the paper envelope without touching it.

"What's that?" Kate asked.

Handwritten in the bottom right corner was the name "Ariadne." Vail bent closer to it and held the flashlight at an angle so he could see the paper around the writing. He looked up at the sprinkler head again. "It's good news and bad news. See if you can find a plastic bag somewhere, something big enough to carry this packet in."

Kate wanted to ask Vail what he thought was inside the envelope, but she also wanted to spend as little time as possible inside the house. She hurried to the back, and Vail could hear her opening and closing drawers. She returned and handed him a torn plastic grocery bag. "This is all I could find. What is that?"

He picked up the packet, using the bag to grip it. "Something I suspect I don't want touching my skin." He flexed the packet. "It feels like a disc packed in powder."

"Do you think Calculus left it?"

"I know he did."

"How?"

Just then they heard a car pull up next to the house. "Go see what that is," he told her while he carefully wrapped the envelope in the bag. Cautiously, Kate went to the window and peeked outside. "This can't be good," she said in a strained whisper.

"Who is it?"

"Best guess is the Russian embassy's SWAT team. Three guys in cheap suits and bad haircuts, pulling down ski masks and carrying large black automatics."

Vail reached over to the circuit-breaker box and threw all the switches to the "off" position. "Quick, go turn on all the light switches."

"What?" Kate asked in an incredulous whisper.

"I've cut the power. Go!"

Vail headed in the opposite direction, flipping up wall switches. Just as the house door opened, they both had made it back to the concealed room, and Vail closed the panel door quietly. Kate drew her weapon and eased back the slide far enough to confirm that a round was in the chamber.

Even though the small room was soundproofed, they could hear the three men moving roughly through the house, occasionally calling out to one another in a foreign language. Their footsteps eventually slowed, and they started talking in lower tones. It sounded like they were now just outside the hidden room. Kate knew that if they were from the embassy, they would be aware of the room and would check it before leaving. A set of footsteps started toward them, and Vail wrapped his arms around Kate, pulling her over to the wall where the circuit breakers were located. He held her a little tighter and then flipped all the circuit breakers as fast as he could.

Instantly there was a series of explosions, and fire flashed under the panel door briefly. The men screamed and ran for the front door. Still holding Kate, Vail punched open the panel entrance and said, "Out the back window." Suddenly the overhead sprinklers kicked on and soaked both of them as they ran to the rear of the house.

Kate reached the window, pulled it open, and climbed out. Vail followed her and closed it behind them. They hurried into the cover of the woods. The night air seemed twice as cold now that their hair and clothing were wet. As soon as they got into the car, Vail started it, revving the engine to boost the temperature. He went to the trunk and retrieved Kate's sweat suit and then waited outside while she changed. When he finally climbed back in, he was shaking. Kate said, "Tell me that part again about how nothing can go wrong."

"They got there fifteen minutes after us, so they

didn't come from D.C. That leaves a distinct possibility that Calculus is talking. They must have come here to retrieve the disc." Vail turned the car around and headed back toward the highway.

"Then why would they come with ski masks and guns drawn?" she asked.

"If Calculus talked, he had to tell them that he'd left a clue for us. Maybe they were just being overly cautious in case we were there."

"Well, they'll know we were there now that we tried to blow up the place."

"Especially when they don't find the disc," Vail said. "That's why we have to get this package processed as quickly as possible. I assume you can have someone from the lab meet us as soon as we get back."

"What kind of examination are you talking about?"

"Chemical."

They pulled onto the highway, and Kate adjusted the heater. "Okay, now that we have time, what's with the packet? 'Good news and bad.' What did you mean? And how did you know that Calculus left it?"

"The first clue was the gunpowder in the lights. Since he's an engineer, Calculus would have known that as an antipersonnel mine it would inflict just minor wounds, because the only projectiles would have been the bulb's glass, which would have broken into very small fragments."

"Then why would he rig them?"

"Besides the explosion and the flying glass, what else happened?"

"The fireball from the explosion, which would probably have caught some things on fire if it hadn't been for the sprinklers."

"Exactly, the sprinklers. That was his purpose. When I saw the bowl directly under the heads in that hidden room, it didn't seem right. The ink on the outside of the packet had caused the paper to deteriorate slightly. I think it's made of water-soluble paper, so when it got wet, it would expose whatever powder is inside to more water. I think his intention was for us to destroy the disc."

"Why would he direct us to the disc and then want to destroy it?"

"If he was still here to work with us on the list, he would have told us about the booby-trapped lights and the powder. But he put them in place so if the Russians somehow got onto him, we would hopefully beat them to the disc and unwittingly destroy it so they would have no proof against him. And if the Russians got there first, and he didn't tell them about the lights, they would destroy it."

"How's a plastic disc going to be destroyed by water?"

"There's also the powder. Did you have high-school chemistry?"

"No."

"I think it's potassium, which when exposed to water has a violent chemical reaction. It would have turned the disc into liquid plastic. That was the bad news, but since we got it without any damage, that leaves the good news."

"Which is?" she asked.

"That he wrote the name 'Ariadne' on it."

"Who's that?"

"It's from Greek mythology. She was the lover of Theseus, who volunteered to kill the Minotaur, a creature that was part man and part bull. It was kept in this complex maze from which it would have been impossible for Theseus to escape after killing it. So Ariadne gave him a golden cord to find his way out. In Logic, there's a process referred to as Ariadne's thread. It's used to describe the solving of a problem that has a number of ways to proceed."

"So that means what?"

"I'm hoping Calculus's choice of 'Ariadne' means there's a subtle set of clues for us to follow from mole to mole."

"But he wanted to sell each name to us, one at a time. Why would he link them all together with the possibility of our being able to find them on our own?"

"Let's not forget he tried to get us to destroy the first clue and any others that might have evolved from it so the Russians couldn't retrieve them to use against him. We weren't supposed to come out of that house with the disc unless he was controlling the situation. Again, it's like the maze: Even if you killed the Minotaur, your punishment was that you'd never be able to find your way out. And as far as why he would provide a link from one to the others, he's a smart guy, probably smarter than his pay grade.

"Most spies have one thing in common," he continued. "They believe they're underpromoted and underappreciated. They have contempt for everyone around them. Maybe he put the link in there to prove how much smarter he is than everyone else—the Russians because he's selling their secrets under their noses and the FBI because we had the answer and didn't realize it. Probably after he'd led us to the moles one by one, he would have exposed how they were all linked together, thereby proving how inept *we* are. It's like some serial killers. They're compelled to send solid but subtle clues to the newspaper and the authorities as to their real identity. And when they're caught by some other means, the media will look at the clues and say, 'How could the police not have figured it out?' Then, even after they're caught, they have eternal revenge against the legal system by letting everyone second-guess the cops' inability to decode the 'obvious.' It's all about control and ego."

"Maybe he was hoping that if something went wrong and we were able to follow the string on our own, we'd do the honorable thing and send the money off to Chicago?" Kate said.

"Actually, that's a more pragmatic analysis than mine. This is America—maybe he thought we would do the right thing."

"So if there is a cord, not only will we have evidence on that disc of Pollock's spying, there'll also be a lead to the next mole."

"Unless I'm wrong."

She adjusted the heat vent so the air blew directly on her soaking hair and started running her fingers through it, trying to dry it. "Don't be absurd. You, wrong? That hasn't happened, for . . . what? Almost fifteen minutes?"

SIX

IT WAS ALMOST 11 P.M. BY THE TIME VAIL CHANGED CLOTHES, and he and Kate drove back to FBI headquarters. At the lab Nate Wilhelm introduced himself as being from the Chemical Unit. Vail took out the plastic-bag-wrapped packet and handed it to him. "We think there's a disc inside the envelope and that it's covered with some water-catalyst powder, possibly potassium, meant to destroy it," Kate said. "The envelope appears to be water-soluble, too."

Wilhelm pulled on a pair of thick latex gloves. "Do you need to preserve the package for prints or handwriting?"

Vail looked at Kate. She said, "Just to be on the safe side, you'd better try."

The examiner put on a pair of safety glasses and a dust mask. Then, with an X-Acto knife, he slit open the end of the envelope. Careful not to drag out any more powder than necessary, he used a pair of padded forceps to remove the disc from the paper container. He took the packet to another workstation and shook out all the powder he could. Then he put a small amount of it into a test tube. Using a pipette, he dripped a couple ounces of water into the tube. The powder bubbled furiously. "It looks like potassium, and it reacts to water like potassium."

He pulled off the gloves and put on a fresh pair, going back to the disc. He dusted it off with a large fingerprint brush, then held it up to the light. "No latents." Out of a box that dispensed them, he took a sterile cloth and wiped the disc off on both sides. He did it twice more with fresh cloths and then took off his mask, glasses, and gloves. "That should do it."

Vail took it by the edges and touched his fingertip to the non-play side of the disc, testing it for any reaction to the moisture from his hand. There was none. He asked Wilhelm for a plastic protective sleeve and dropped it into his side jacket pocket.

Kate said, "Nate, we don't want this to show up on any paperwork. Will that cause you any problems?"

"Less paperwork is never a problem, Kate."

"Thanks."

As Kate and Vail started toward the elevator, he said, "Should we wait until tomorrow to see what's on this?"

"Like you could wait."

He laughed. "I was just trying to see how tired you were."

When the elevator door opened, the only passenger, a black man, said, "Steve Vail?"

It was Luke Bursaw, an agent Vail had worked with in Detroit more than five years earlier. "Luke," Vail said, shaking hands with him. "What are *you* doing here?"

"I finally got my 'office of preference' transfer. I'm at the Washington Field Office now, working general criminal. Are you back with the Bureau?"

Vail looked at Kate. "I'm sorry. This is Kate Bannon. She's—"

"Sure, I remember Kate from Detroit. And now she's a deputy assistant director. We get most of the memos over at WFO. How are you, Kate?" He extended his hand.

Kate took it. She remembered him because he was the only agent Vail had worked with in Detroit, usually when a difficult arrest needed to be made. The most memorable one was where Vail and Bursaw came barging into the office with four bank robbers handcuffed together early one morning. One of them, also wanted for murder, had been on Michigan's ten-most-wanted list. It happened shortly after she'd arrived in Detroit, and the thing that had always stuck with her was that no one seemed to think it was out of the ordinary, at least not for Vail.

Bursaw had gone to Penn on a wrestling scholarship and majored in philosophy. He'd gained a couple of pounds since she'd last seen him, but he still seemed to move with an athlete's ease. "And I remember you, Luke. What brings a WFO agent here at this time of night?"

"I caught a couple of shifts as night supervisor that nobody wanted—you know, holiday pay. And I had some evidence to drop off at the lab on the way home." Bursaw turned back to Vail. "One thing I do know about you, Steve, is how good you were at ducking questions. So what are you doing here?"

"Actually, I am back with the Bureau, sort of as an independent contractor, working with Kate."

Bursaw glanced at him carefully, letting Vail know that there were still holes in his story that would be queried later. "Small world. Where are you staying?"

"Over on Sixteenth Street."

"Any chance we could get together? Share some lies over a beer?"

"Sure. I'll give you a call."

"Actually, I've got a problem, and you're the perfect person to run it by."

"What kind of problem?"

"A woman from headquarters, an intelligence analyst, went missing a few months back, and I wound up with the case. So far I'm getting nowhere."

Vail took the DVD out of his jacket and handed it to Kate. "Any reason this can't wait until morning?" he asked her.

"It can wait. Besides, I am beat."

"We'll get a running start at it first thing tomorrow."

"Sure." The elevator opened onto the first floor, and the two men got out. "Nice seeing you, Luke."

"You too, Kate."

As they walked toward the street exit, Bursaw said, "Any idea how long you're going to be here?"

"To tell you the truth, it's starting to look like the minute I stepped off the plane, I'd already been here too long."

• • •

VAIL AND BURSAW found a bar that wasn't far from headquarters. Since it was relatively empty, they went to the far end and climbed onto a couple of stools. After the bartender had brought them beer, Bursaw asked, "So what could possibly have brought you back to the Bureau after the way they treated you?"

"You know you're one of the few people I ever trusted."

"I can't really remember you trusting anyone. Sounds like you're about to tell me that you can't tell me."

"If you knew what this was about, you'd thank me for not involving you, especially when they start hooking people up to the polygraph."

"That serious?"

"I think you know I wouldn't be keeping it from you if it weren't."

Bursaw nodded and then took a sip of beer. "You're right, I don't want to know. But how did *you* get involved in it?"

"I did some work for the director six months ago, in L.A."

"That Pentad thing, that was you?"

"More Kate than me. I was just looking for a change of pace."

"From the little I heard, you got it—and then some." Bursaw looked at him for some reaction, but Vail just shrugged. "You never did like a lot of noise." Bursaw chuckled salaciously. "But you and Kate, huh? That's got to be a major factor in you being dragged back in."

Vail snorted. "It was supposed to be, but unfortunately we don't seem to be a good fit."

"You know what Nietzsche said—'Woman was God's second blunder.'"

"Is that a shot at me or at Kate?"

Bursaw took a scholarly tone. "Philosophy is not a discipline of answers but one of contemplation."

"Great, things aren't surreal enough around here. Now I've got a black guy quoting Hitler's favorite philosopher."

"Whether it's working or not, that's still a good-looking woman," Bursaw said.

"She is that," Vail said. "But enough about my blundering celibacy. What's the story on the missing employee?"

"Her name is Sundra Boston. She's an intelligence analyst at headquarters, or at least she was. I didn't know her. She disappeared about three months before I was transferred back here. I've got this cousin, Eden. Nice gal, but she married a loser. Actually, 'drunk' would be a more accurate description. They got a couple of kids, and he's always going off on these drinking binges, leaving her with nothing to get by on. Anyway, she met Sundra at church, and they became friends. My cousin may have made a couple of bad choices in her life, but she's not a complainer. When her husband takes off, she sucks it up and doesn't say anything to anyone. I suppose it's as much out of embarrassment as anything else. She said that somehow Sundra always seemed to know when she was going through those times, and she would show up unannounced at Eden's with a carload of groceries. She'd been doing it for over a year. When I got back here, Eden pulled me aside at a family get-together and asked me if I could find out what happened to her. She thought Sundra had been transferred to some secret assignment or something.

"So I checked indices and found that we had a case on her disappearance, and that it was being handled on my squad. I'd been back in D.C. less than two weeks, knew nothing about the case, and I hadn't caught on to my supervisor yet. So I went in and asked him about it." Bursaw shook his head and took a long pull on his beer. "Steve, this guy is everything that is wrong with the new Bureau. He actually grew up in Beverly Hills—that's right, my brother, 90210—and couldn't get through an hour of the day without performing some affectation. He calls the bad guys 'thugs' and 'hoodlums.' When I asked him about Sundra, he gave me the rundown and told me that the investigation was at a standstill. Then he cocks his head to the side in thought and says, 'You know, she's an African-American, too. You could probably find her, because these people would talk to you.' And you think the leadership was bad when you were in. Then he reassigns the case to me as if he had just had some sort of movie-of-the-week life-altering epiphany."

"I take it you haven't had any luck getting those African-Americans to tell you where she is?"

Bursaw grinned. "Don't start," he said. "So I pull the file and find out that very little had been done after the first thirty days. I made up my mind right there to jump on it with both feet."

"Not to belittle your altruism, but what does she look like?"

"You're right, she is good-looking. Which doesn't hurt. But I figure with what she did for my cousin, she must be a good person and deserves to have someone searching for her for real."

"A Bureau employee disappears and no one is making it a priority?"

"At first they did have the full-court press on it, but when they found that she was in major debt . . . well, like you always said, they prefer the theory that requires the least amount of work. So they decided that she probably just took off for parts unknown and changed her name or got married or both so she could wipe the slate clean."

"Define 'major debt.'"

"Almost fifty K on credit cards alone."

"Isn't it hard to run up a bill that big without enjoying some of society's moral taboos?"

"You don't spend much money, do you, Steve? Even though you won't read it in the file, I think that's what they thought," Bursaw said. "It wasn't drugs. She'd just had a physical and been screened. And all her phone records and credit-card receipts have been checked, so it's unlikely that she had a gambling problem. But she did like nice things. She'd recently bought a house and had a nice car. From what I've been told, she always dressed much better than the rest of us government humps. With that kind of taste, fifty thousand isn't such a big leap."

"So they're trying to put it to sleep, and you're going to make them pay for it by embarrassing them with their ineptness."

"I would like nothing better, but I'm not sure anyone will notice."

"You haven't changed much, Luke."

Bursaw smiled slowly. "As if I have to explain the joys of belittling management to you. The good news is that I'm not getting any pressure to solve it. The bad news is, there's something wrong with it that I can't figure out."

"Wrong how?"

"Okay, let's assume she took off to get out from under that debt. The search-warrant inventory at her house showed that she left everything there, and I mean everything. She had a fairly new laptop computer. It was still there. Seven-hundred-dollar shoes that hadn't been worn. And for me, maybe the toughest thing to explain, her designer suitcases were still there. The price tags still on them."

"Have you called the locals to see if there've been any other incidents of women missing under similar circumstances?"

"Some sort of serial thing, yeah, I thought of that, but you know what a mess that can start. I do have some feelers out, though."

"When did you last check her credit cards?" Vail said.

"I look at them once a week. Nary a blip anywhere." Bursaw took another sip of his beer. "I'd like you to look at it."

"What is it that you think I can do? I didn't go to an Ivy League school."

"I don't know, maybe I'm on tilt with this. Maybe I'm trying too hard to show the world how smart I am or, more likely, what a moron my supervisor is. I don't know. You were always good at finding things no one else could. Maybe take a look at the file. See if I'm missing anything."

"Right now my days are pretty full."

Bursaw gave him an easy grin. "How are your nights?"

"With everything I've got going on, I would have to be a blithering idiot to say yes."

Bursaw drained his beer. "Then let's go take a look at the file."

IT WAS A little after nine when Kate got to the off-site the next morning. She was surprised when she heard the shower going. Evidently Vail had slept in. She made a pot of coffee and, when it was ready, poured herself a cup. In the observation room, she started reviewing the information Vail had pinned to the wall. A few minutes later, he walked out of the kitchen and held up his cup. "Thanks."

"You and Luke reminiscing over too many beers last night?"

"Actually we were at WFO until about four A.M. reviewing the case file on his missing analyst."

"I thought you didn't like this work."

"I like the work just fine. In fact, it's the reason I dislike the people who keep getting in the way of it."

"That sounds more like a rationalization than a defense, Vail."

"Of all the times Luke helped me in Detroit— and some of them were pretty touch and go—the guy never once asked me for a favor. Until last night."

"Sorry. It's just that I would have thought you had enough to do."

"I guess that's when you find out if someone is truly worth your friendship."

"Were you able to help him?"

"I gave him a few suggestions. I'm not sure he needed them. He's not the guy I'd want after me," Vail said. "You ready to watch that disc? Or did you peek last night, Katie?"

"No." She took it out of her briefcase. "But I was a little surprised you trusted me with it."

"It wasn't me trusting you that was the problem—it was me trusting me if I held on to it."

She laughed cynically. "Oh, honesty. Is that your latest tactic to deceive me?"

"I figured if anything would keep you off balance, it would be telling the truth. Apparently that's not going to work either."

She set the disc in the DVD player. On the monitor screen, they recognized the meeting room at the Denton safe house. It was followed by a couple of seconds of static and then by someone holding a hand-printed sign in front of the camera. On it were written the date, the time, and the name Charles Dennis Pollock. "That should eliminate any guesswork about who's starring in this little production."

Another few seconds of static were followed by two men sitting in the room. Pollock, recognizable from his security-background photo, was unknowingly facing the camera. He opened a briefcase that was on the floor next to him and handed a sheaf of papers to the other man. In turn, the man, who carefully never let any of his face be exposed, handed Pollock three bundles of bills and then in heavily accented English demanded, more than requested, that it be counted. While Pollock obliged, the handler deliberately held up the documents he had received and slowly paged through them so they could be captured on video. Several had CLASSIFIED stamped across them. Pollock then placed the money in his briefcase. A brief discussion ensued about what other material Pollock could provide. The screen again went to static. Vail fast-forwarded it until the end. There was nothing else on it.

"That's it? What about the golden thread or whatever you call it?"

"The golden cord," Vail said. "I don't know."

"Maybe Calculus was just screwing with us and wrote 'Ariadne' on the envelope to frustrate us so we'd be willing to pay more."

"That's a possibility. Spies do love mind games. Maybe Pollock somehow has the answer to whoever's next. There's only one way to find out."

"You want to arrest him?".

"That does seem to be the next logical step now that we have irrefutable evidence that he's a spy."

"Then I've got to let Bill Langston know."

"Come on, Kate. You know that finding the next name is going to be tough enough without going through the *system*."

"Even you can't arrest someone for espionage without somebody somewhere authorizing it. There's no other way but the *system*. Finding out who Pollock is and that he's a spy has brought us back into the aboveground world of rules and— God forbid—the law."

It was moments like this that reminded Vail he'd been correct in choosing a life in which he answered to no one. And since Kate had told him that a relationship with her was no longer possible—everything else being equal—he would have gone off on his own and done whatever he needed to do to resolve the situation with this man who had committed treason. But the only reason, or at least the deciding one, he'd taken this assignment was to help Kate regain her reputation. "How about if we just interview Pollock? If he doesn't cooperate, *I'll* call Langston for authorization. But first I want a chance to find out if he has the key to the next name before he disappears into a bureaucratic maze that in all likelihood will shut this down. With Calculus gone, it looks like he's our only shot."

"What are you going to do if he does cooperate, leave him out there?"

"If he's cooperative, we'll ask him to take a ride and hand-deliver him to Langston so he can take all the bows. That'll keep him happy, and hopefully we'll have the next clue."

"So either way, by the end of the day Langston will be notified."

"If that's what you want, absolutely."

"I really hate it when you start a promise with 'if.'" She studied his face briefly for signs of deception. As usual there were none. "Okay, but I'm driving. That way I can abandon you at the first sign of trouble."

Vail laughed. "That off-ramp was three or four exits ago."

SEVEN

KATE FOUND A PARKING SPACE NEAR THE MAIN ENTRANCE of Alliant Industries in Calverton, Virginia, Pollock's employer. Vail opened the folder containing the information they'd printed from Pollock's security investigation and dialed the work number, holding the phone so Kate could hear. "Charles Pollock, please."

"I'm sorry, he's not in today."

Vail looked at Kate apprehensively. "This is Hank Bass, I'm a friend of his. Could you tell him I called?"

"Certainly, sir."

"Wait a minute, I've got his home number. Will I be able to reach him there?"

"I'm sorry, Mr. Bass, I'm not sure."

"Don't bother with the message. I'll track him down." Vail thanked her and hung up.

"That can't be good. It sounds like he didn't call in. Maybe we should get some help and put on a full-court press."

"Normally I'd say that made sense, but don't forget, if we're right about Calculus giving everyone up, the Russians could be moving Pollock out of here right now. Proper channels would slow us down and ensure his getting away. Let's try his house. Maybe he's just taking a day off."

Kate stared past him for a few seconds. "God help me, I think I may need some sort of therapy, because that actually makes sense to me."

CHARLES POLLOCK'S HOUSE was surprisingly large but in a state of advanced disrepair. It was a half-timbered Tudor and in need of a fresh coat of paint. A front gutter hung by one end, angling across the first-floor windows. The second-floor stucco had some deep cracks in it and was chipping off. Weeds were over a foot high and frozen upright in the lawn. As the two agents pulled in to the driveway, there was a stillness that made Vail wary.

He got to the door first and unbuttoned his topcoat, hitting the thumb release on his holster. Gently he pushed Kate behind him. He knocked loudly. After a few seconds, he put his ear against the door and listened. "Can you check for his car?"

Kate went over to the attached garage and peered into the window. "Empty." Vail watched her as he continued to listen for movement inside. She cupped her hand over her eyes to cut the sun's glare and searched the garage's interior. "The inside house door is open. As cold as it is outside, that can't be intentional."

Vail walked over and pulled up the overhead door, drawing his Glock. Kate slipped hers out of the holster in response. They walked into the garage, and he pushed the door leading into the house completely open.

Once in the kitchen, they listened for anyone moving around. "Hello!" Vail yelled. When there was no response, he nodded toward the doorway leading to the rest of the house, and without another word he and Kate swept from room to room, covering each other. "Okay, do you want the upstairs or the basement?" he asked.

"Basement."

They split up, each heading for a different set of stairs. Five minutes later they were both back to the kitchen, their handguns reholstered. "Do you think he's onto us?" Kate asked.

"Could be, if Calculus is talking. The Russians would most likely warn him then. Or he could just be at the grocery store. We'd better pull back and sit on it until we figure out which."

Kate found a spot almost a block away and parked. She went to the trunk and came back with a pair of binoculars, handing them to Vail. "Pretty high-tech for us, isn't it?" he said.

"I figured it was time to move our little adventures forward into the seventeenth century."

Vail looked at Pollock's house through them. "Nice." Still holding them to his eyes, he turned and scanned Kate up and down. "Very nice." She hit the front of the binoculars, causing them to bang into Vail's eyes. "Ow!"

"I thought you bricklayers were a tough bunch."

"Not us blind bricklayers."

"What are we going to do if Pollock doesn't come home?"

Vail picked up the pages from the suspected spy's

file and leafed through them. "There's a cell-phone number here."

"You want me to call it?"

"I'm not sure how much good that will do us, since we won't know where he's at."

Kate thought for a second. "You want me to have it pinged?"

"As a deputy assistant director, you should be able to get something like that done pretty easily. I mean, there's got to be some advantage to having you along."

"You'd be surprised how there's absolutely no advantage to working with certain highly rated people." She jerked the sheet of paper out of his hand and dialed her cell phone.

It was late in the afternoon before Kate got a callback. She made some notes and hung up. "He had the phone turned off until about an hour ago." She started the car and handed Vail her notes. "Just west of McLean. Those are the coordinates. If you've recovered your eyesight, please punch them into the GPS."

DAYLIGHT WAS FADING as Kate pulled over. "Do you think that's it?"

Vail glanced at the dashboard locator. "It's the only building within a half mile."

They were looking at an ancient ten-story brick building. Kate was on her phone again, calling the McLean police to find out what the structure was. After waiting for a while, she made some more notes and hung up. "It's some sort of historical building that housed World War One wounded soldiers who were brought back here to recuperate. After the war it was turned into a government warehouse. Because its heating and electrical were so out of date and rehabbing it would have been too expensive, they were going to tear it down. But then the historical people got involved. They started filing injunctions, and it's been going back and forth for longer than anyone can remember."

"Why would Pollock be in there? It doesn't make any sense," Vail said.

"Maybe he was just parked here when he made the call."

"Why don't you see if there've been any calls since the first one."

Kate called headquarters again and, after being on hold for a couple of minutes, hung up. "Nothing. They're going to check it every fifteen minutes and let us know if there's a change."

When they hadn't heard anything an hour later, Vail opened the car door and said, "I'll be right back."

"Where are you going?"

"To see if there's a way into that place."

"You think he could actually be in there?"

"If there's no way in, then we'll know he's not. At least we won't have to sit here the rest of the night."

Kate said, "I'm going to call his house and see if I get an answer."

Ten minutes later Vail got back into the car. "I take it he's not at home."

"No answer."

"I found a way in."

"What does that mean?"

"Could have been just kids breaking in. Hard to tell." He picked up the binoculars and used them to explore the building's windows. After a few minutes, he said, "There! On the fifth floor. Did you see it? A light, and then it disappeared."

"You're sure?"

"Yes. Let's go."

Taking a flashlight, Vail led the way around the back of the building to a door that had been carefully jimmied open and then closed, giving the appearance that it was still secure. He pushed his fingers into the narrow crack on one side of the door and pulled on the edge until he worked it free. They both stepped inside. Vail stopped and listened. He snapped on the flashlight. "I think the stairway is straight ahead."

Kate followed him in the semidarkness, occasionally stepping on something soft that she hoped were articles of abandoned clothing. Then they started climbing the stairs.

At each landing Vail stopped and listened, every so often turning to look at her. "You okay?" he whispered with uncharacteristic concern.

"Yeah, fine. You?"

He smiled. "I'm okay."

When they reached the landing between the third and fourth floors, he stood motionless for a good five minutes. Kate could see that Vail sensed there was going to be trouble—and it was going to be soon. Her suspicion was confirmed when he drew his automatic. She did the same. As cold as it was, she felt a bead of sweat work its way down her spine. Slowly, Vail stepped onto the next stair.

On the fifth floor, they could see as some light from the street seeped in through a hallway window. Vail swept the floor with his flashlight to make sure there was nothing underfoot that might announce their arrival. The creaking floor was bad enough. He walked forward to the door of the room he thought he'd seen the brief flash of light come from. The number 508, painted on it in gold-edged black paint, had all but peeled off. Standing to the side, he tried the knob. The door was unlocked. He looked at Kate to see if she was ready, and she gripped her weapon with both hands. Vail turned the knob and pushed the door open.

It was pitch-black inside, no ambient light anywhere. Still at the side of the door and without being able to see in, he flashed the light into the room to see if it would draw fire. It didn't. He motioned for Kate to stay where she was. He turned off the flashlight, took a deep breath, and stepped into the room. Quickly he moved to the side so he wasn't outlined by the light coming from the hallway. He looked back and could see Kate leaning into the room. When he didn't give her any instructions, she moved into the room and stepped from in front of the door as well. Vail held his light as far to the side as he could and turned it on. Other than some scattered debris on the floor, the room was empty. Ahead of him was another closed door to another room. They both moved to opposite sides of the door, and Vail opened it.

He flashed the light in and saw Charles Pollock

slumped in the corner of the room. A syringe was stuck in his arm, and his throat had been cut.

Before entering, Vail scanned the light around the room, because he could see that Pollock had been dead for a while and couldn't have been responsible for the light Vail had seen from the street. There was another door. He and Kate entered the room and felt something sticky on the soles of their shoes. He moved the light to the floor and could see that it was blood in an inordinately large pool, starting to coagulate. Vail noted that there were no drag marks from there to the corner where Pollock's body was now propped up. They went over to him.

Vail pulled the syringe out of Pollock's arm and held it up to the flashlight. "The color of the residue looks too dark to be heroin."

Suddenly a burst of gunfire came through the unexplored door. Both agents dove to the floor. Vail opened fire, letting his Glock stitch the door as he emptied the magazine. He rolled back into a safe position, dropped the empty magazine, and jammed in a fresh one, letting the slide go home.

He nodded to Kate, and she knew what he wanted. She fired a half-dozen rounds slowly at the door while he crawled forward. He pulled himself up against the wall next to it and pointed his automatic at the doorway as Kate got to her feet, rushed forward, and pinned herself against the wall on the opposite side of the door. Vail pushed it open, again trying to draw fire. None came.

He rolled around the doorjamb, his automatic at eye level. A hole large enough for a person to escape had been cut through an adjoining wall. "Come on."

She followed him as he went back the way they'd come and into the hall, running to the stairwell. He opened the door and listened for whoever it was that had shot at them. Kate could hear faint footsteps. Vail's head cocked to the side in disbelief. "He's going to the roof."

Taking the stairs two at a time, Vail tried to close the gap. Kate was right behind him, pushing a fresh magazine into her automatic as she ran. Then they heard a door slam.

When they got to the roof entrance, the door was closed. The lock had been taken out, leaving a two-inch circular hole in the steel door. Vail pushed on it carefully, but it would not give. "He's blocked it with something." With measured force, he bounced his shoulder against it, testing its resistance. "There's some give." He stood back and kicked it hard, but it held. He took two more steps back and leaped forward, landing his foot where he thought the device was holding it closed. He did it again, and still the door remained blocked.

Kate said, "Do you smell smoke?"

Vail turned toward the stairs and inhaled. He holstered his gun and grabbed Kate's hand. "Let's get out of here." When they got down to the next floor, he could smell gasoline mixed in with the choking odor of the smoke. He looked over the railing and could see that the stairwell two floors below was engulfed in flames. "Back to the roof."

When they got to the door again, Kate said, "Can't we shoot it open?"

"I doubt it, it's steel, and whatever is jamming it is below the lock hole." Once more he took a couple of steps back and this time charged the door, ramming his shoulder into it, but it held. "I have to find some way to get a little more into it. It's close to going." He grabbed her by the arm and pulled her to his side. "We've got to ram into it as one body. When I say go, keep pasted against me so our weights combine into one. Ready?"

She drew her hips up so they were touching his and nodded.

"Go!" Vail said, and they lunged at the door. Their timing was a little off. Vail hit it first and a fraction of a second later she slammed into his ribs. Both of them stepped back a couple of strides, and he said, "Again . . . set . . . go!" This try their timing was in sync, and there was a loud wooden crack as the door flew open. They both fell over the threshold.

"I'll check for a fire escape. Call 911," he said.

Vail ran to the side of the building he hadn't seen before breaking in. When he came back, Kate was giving the address to the emergency operator. She looked at him anxiously. He said, "There are no fire escapes."

EIGHT

THE TALL, SLENDER MAN WITH THE SPLAYED NOSE SAT behind the wheel and watched as one of his men lowered himself carefully down a rope that hung from the roof of the burning building. A second man came from around the back of the building and stood underneath until the first man was safely on the ground. Once he was, the two of them looked up before casually walking back to the waiting black SUV. They got into the backseat without saying a word. One of them smelled of gasoline and smoke. Sitting next to the driver was the big man with the eyes that barely moved. "Was either of them shot?" he asked in a heavy accent.

"I'm not sure. Possibly," answered the man who had come down the rope.

"Which means they weren't," the driver said, his voice both apologetic and angry.

The passenger shifted himself in the seat and watched the top of the building as smoke continued to pour out of it. "It will be more entertaining this way."

"THEN HOW DID the guy we chased get off the roof?" Kate asked.

Vail saw what looked like a cable hanging over the side of the building. They both went over and examined it. It was about thirty feet long but was tied to a much longer rope. Both together were long enough to reach to within ten feet of the ground. "That's how." The end of the cable was anchored in a nearby water drain. Vail pulled on it, testing his weight against it. "Think you can make it?"

She looked back at the smoke billowing out of the door they had forced open. "You mean there're other choices?"

Holding on to the cable, she was starting to climb over the low wall when he said, "Hang on a minute." He went back and closed the door. The smoke started streaming out of the cracks around it and from the lock hole. He picked up the now-broken board that had been snapped in half when he and Kate forced open the door. It was a length of two-by-two that had been jammed against a short section of two-by-four nailed to the roof. The two-by-four had a notch cut into it to hold one end of the two-by-two in place. The other end had been notched also and jammed up under the door handle. "If they'd used a two-by-four, we'd still be in there."

"Maybe they didn't have any."

"Two-by-fours are a lot easier to find than two-by-twos."

"At the risk of sounding like I'm giving you an order, can we discuss this on the ground?"

Vail walked back to the braided cable and examined it more closely. He took out his lockback knife and opened it. "Are you still carrying that thing?" she asked.

Carefully, he cut into one of the strands and sniffed it. He looked at her soberly. "It's det cord."

"Det cord as in detonation cord?"

"I've seen it on demolition jobs. When it's ignited at one end, it explodes so fast you can't tell which end was set off."

"Why would they use that?"

"That's something we have to figure out before we go any further." He got down on his knees next to the drain that the end of the cable disappeared into. "Let me have that flashlight." He tried to pull the drain cover off. When it wouldn't budge, he said, "It's been spot-welded." He got closer and used the light to peer down into the small crack surrounding the cable. After a few seconds, he stood up and snapped the light off with finality.

"What is it?"

Vail didn't answer right away but instead looked over the side of the building and tugged easily on the braided cord.

"What is it?"

"There's a device connected to the end. Det cord is set off with a blasting cap. There's one of those in there, too. There's also a battery and a large, heavy-duty spring. What happens is when there's enough weight on the cable and rope, the metal spring lengthens and makes contact, closing the circuit between the battery and the blasting cap, which in turn sets off the det cord. If we're both hanging on it ten stories up—*poof.* It's gone, and so are we."

"But whoever was shooting at us used it."

"We never got a look at him. We don't know how

much he weighed. He could have been a hundred and thirty pounds for all we know."

"How much do you weigh?" she asked.

"One-ninety. What are you, about one-eighty?"

"One-thirty-five, Vail."

He got down on his knees again and turned on the flashlight. He took a few extra seconds looking into the thin opening before getting up. "You should be all right."

"What about you?"

"They had to build some tolerance into it. I'm guessing that to open that spring up fully and set it off, both of us would have to be on it together. You go first. Once you're down, I'll get on it."

In the distance Kate could hear the sirens now. "Maybe we should wait for the fire department."

"They haven't got anything that can reach ten floors." He squatted down and put his hand flat on the deck. "It's getting hot. We don't have that much time."

Kate went over to the side and grabbed the cable. Vail could see the uncertainty in her eyes. "I could be wrong about how much weight this can hold. Maybe you should take off your clothes just to be safe."

She got a new grip on the cable. "Vail, I'd rather do a two-and-a-half into the concrete." She slipped over the side and looped the cord around her foot as a brake to control the speed of her descent.

FROM THE BLACK vehicle, the four men watched Kate come over the side of the roof and wrap the cable over her foot. As she started down, all of them looked back anxiously at the roof to see where the second agent was.

Suddenly it seemed as if the sirens doubled in volume. The driver's eyes darted over to his passenger, but he was still watching the roofline intently. The sirens grew even louder.

The driver started the engine as a plea to leave. The passenger snorted in disappointment and then turned forward in his seat and closed his eyes. The SUV made a U-turn and drove away just below the speed limit.

AS SOON AS Kate let go of the rope and dropped the last few feet, Vail was over the side as fast as possible. Just as he reached the ground, a fire truck pulled up, and Vail told the crew about the explosive cord. "The fire shouldn't detonate it, but if it does, I don't think it'll hurt anyone inside the building. It's only the upper thirty feet or so."

Kate and Vail went to their car to get out of the way. He started to say something, and she held up her hand. "Not a word until I call Bill Langston."

"Okay, but I can tell you he's—"

She thrust her hand at him to demand his silence as she dialed. Without supplying any details, she told the assistant director that they had identified Pollock and how they tracked him down, finding him dead. She told him about escaping from the burning building and that the fire department was there now trying to extinguish it. At last she said, "I'll be here," and hung up. "If you were planning to say he's not going to be happy, congratulations on your extraordinary understanding of the human mind."

"Just for that, next burning building you can stay home."

"This isn't funny, Steve. I'm not letting you talk me into anything like this again."

"You act like it's the worst thing I've ever done to you. How about when I stole the three million dollars from your safe? And you didn't know what I was doing and, even worse, where I was so you could yell at me."

She finally smiled. "Okay, that was worse."

"And what happened? You were a hero, even got invited to the Irish ambassador's New Year's party. Of course, I got the best night of my life out of it."

She turned to him and searched his face for a moment. "I bet you say that to all the women you seduce with sculpture."

"Less than half, I swear."

Kate laughed. "You'd better let me handle Langston when he gets here."

"That's the best offer I've gotten all day."

"Enjoy it, because that's the *only* offer you're going to get all day. And by 'all day' I mean ever again."

"You say that now, but a few more dead bodies, another shoot-out or two, maybe an explosion, and you'll be putty in my hands."

Kate stared out the windshield for a moment. "I guess there's no doubt now that the Russians have Calculus talking. But why kill Pollock? And why try to kill us?"

"Think about what would have happened if their plan had succeeded. The det cord would have exploded, leaving us dead on the ground with a rope that would have appeared to have come untied. For lack of a better explanation, it would have looked like we ineptly started a fire to destroy evidence. Inside was a murdered spy whose blood was all over both our shoes. Not only do the Russians no longer have to worry about what Pollock might tell us, but the Bureau gets a huge black eye out of it."

Kate said, "That seems a little drastic, but maybe the Russians have decided to play hardball. Didn't Calculus say something about how they were under orders not to get caught spying?"

"There's only one reason they would have gone to all that trouble—it's the disc. The way we snuck into the safe house, they probably figured the two of us were freelancing. And then again tonight it was just the two of us. If we're sneaking around on the Bureau, they probably assumed—correctly—that no one else knows about the disc. If they got rid of us, they don't have to worry about it. Which means there's something else on it that leads to the next spy."

"That's a lot of supposition, Steve."

"There's one way to find out. We need to take another look at the DVD."

Thirty minutes later Bill Langston pulled up next to their car; his deputy, John Kalix, was driving. Vail said to Kate, "We can't let him know about the disc."

"That shouldn't be a problem, since I'm not sure *I* believe it contains anything. We've already looked at it, remember?"

As Kate started to get out, Vail nodded toward the assistant director and said to her, "Boy, am I glad I'm not in your shoes. He looks mad."

A few minutes later, Kate got back in the car. "He wants to talk to you."

"You told him I was here?"

"We'll see if you still have your sense of humor when you get back."

Vail slid into the rear seat of the assistant director's car. Langston turned around, and his look of displeasure was clear. "I thought you were instructed to keep me advised of any developments."

"You don't think this is a development?"

"I think this is at the end of a chain of developments."

Without mentioning the possible lead to the next mole, Vail answered Langston's questions. He laid out everything that had led them from Calculus's text message to tracking Pollock to how he died. "You broke into a Russian safe house?" Langston thundered.

"That's where the answer was," Vail said, with a calm that was intended to contrast the assistant director's anger.

"You can't do that," Langston said, his voice quieter now but still strained.

"Not the first time I've heard that this week," Vail said. "To keep this civil, I'm going to pretend that you are going to accept what I'm about to say, although I seriously doubt you will. You and I come with two different sets of instructions. Where your methods end, mine begin. I wasn't brought into this because I was likely to follow the agent handbook.

And I'll continue to do what I think is necessary until the director tells me to turn around and go home. Don't take my tactics personally. What I do has only one purpose—to find the answer. It has nothing to do with you."

"I'm not asking you to do things differently. I'm just asking you to keep me informed."

Vail laughed. "Did you really want me to let you know I was going to break into property owned by the Russian embassy?"

It was at that moment Langston realized how foolish he was being. Of course Vail was right. He was taking all the chances, and although Langston wasn't exactly in charge, his division's major problem was being resolved. The time would come when Vail was no longer needed, a time when the assistant director could grab the reins of the investigation from him and claim its success. As though in response to Vail's question, Langston laughed. "I didn't say I wanted to be informed of *everything*."

Vail was surprised at Langston's apparent change of heart. "Good, because right now this is a race between us and the Russians, and they have Calculus, a distinct advantage."

"Your argument is not without merit. But if you do identify any more spies, please let me know. Preferably before you kill them."

Vail started to climb out of the car. "If not before, you're the first one I'll call from the lockup."

Langston watched him get back into his car. He said to Kalix, "What do you think about all this?"

"In the plus column, there's one less spy to deal with. However, he is dead, so there will be no intelligence to come out of it. And politically, because of the director, you have no choice but to give Vail his head. He may well find all these spies if you don't try to control him. But you have to protect yourself if this blows up—which, given the way he operates, it most likely will."

"From now on, John, your number-one priority is to make sure anything that Vail does is not traceable to me. That I had no knowledge of his activities beforehand. If we can manage that, he's got a deputy assistant director at his side, and she'll have to take the hit."

An unmarked police car pulled up, and two detectives got out. Vail went over to them and introduced himself, giving them a brief explanation of what had happened.

"We're going to be at the scene for a while. Can you come in and give us a statement tomorrow morning, say, nine o'clock?" one of them asked, handing Vail a card.

"I'll be there."

KATE AND VAIL had been driving for a few minutes before she said, "You know that when Langston reports to the director that you found the first name on the list, he's going to try to turn it around and blowtorch you."

"The next time you feel the need to ask me why I don't come back to the Bureau, please remember that."

"Believe me, I won't bring it up again," Kate said. "What do you want to do now?"

"Smelling all this smoke, I was thinking barbecue."

Once they got into Washington, it didn't take long to find a neighborhood barbecue restaurant. It was an old place, with sagging wooden floors and rickety Formica tables. The embossed-tin ceiling was stained brown from decades of cooking residue. When Kate and Vail walked in, the place was filled with regulars, who cautiously sized them up at a glance as cops. The house specialties were ribs and brisket. Kate watched the waitress deliver a plate full of meat and fries to an adjoining table and ordered a salad. Vail ordered the brisket.

"What makes you so sure that there's something else on the disc?" she said.

"I can't imagine Calculus leaving that Ariadne clue without there being anything to it. But if Pollock was supposed to supply the next step, we may be finished. Which, if nothing else, will make Langston happy. He'll be able to lay it all off on me, and I'm not sure he'd be wrong."

Kate laughed sarcastically. "Come on, Vail. Contrition? It doesn't come in your size. And surrender? You? What are you planning that you're not telling me about? You're going to break into Pollock's house, aren't you?"

"You're forgetting that I'm just passing through. And although I enjoy being shot at as much as the next guy, one of these fools might actually hit me."

"You were passing through Los Angeles, too."

"I was blinded by your charms."

The waitress brought the food and asked Vail if he needed anything else. He tilted his head playfully and said, "Would you tell my sister here that you can't live on salad?"

The waitress laughed agreeably, handed him the check, and went back to the kitchen.

"Cute," Kate said.

"Sorry. I went weak in the knees from having a woman smile warmly at me."

"It didn't look like your knees from here, bricklayer." She ate a forkful of salad, then said, "So that's it? You can't think of anything else to do?"

"How about we go back and take another look at everything, including the DVD."

She watched as Vail started working his way through the mounds of smoked meat and potatoes. He'd been right about the waitress; she had kept eye contact with him a moment longer than necessary. Kate had seen other women look at him the same way. Although he wasn't particularly handsome, women sensed something about him that was both primal and protective. She had noticed it as far back as Detroit. The night before, in that secret room with the gunmen closing in and Vail about to set off an explosion of unknown intensity, it had never occurred to her that he wouldn't get her out. And it hadn't been any different tonight on that rooftop. The tough times would never be the problem between them. It was the danger, she supposed, that kept them close. But without it, even the simplest date invariably turned contentious.

NINE

WHEN THEY WALKED INTO THE OBSERVATION ROOM AT THE Sixteenth Street off-site, Vail dropped the DVD into the player and said, "We've got to be missing something."

"Why are you so sure there's something to miss? Maybe there are a bunch of clues hidden and Calculus didn't have time to tie them together."

Vail took a few seconds to consider what she'd said. "Good point. Maybe he was waiting to see if we would make the first payment before linking them up. Or maybe the relative at the Chicago bank has the key." Vail picked up the phone.

"What are you doing?"

"I'm calling Langston and having him forward the payment for Pollock to Chicago."

She took the phone from his hand. "I'm not sure he wants to hear from you just yet. I'll call."

Vail watched her as she argued with the assistant director.

"I know he's dead, I was there, remember?"

She glanced at Vail, and he noted an unusual disdain in her eyes.

"This is why Calculus set up the alternative, in case something happened to him," she continued.

"We think there's a possibility that the relative in Chicago may have the key to identifying more of them." Her voice was gradually becoming insistent, its momentum unyielding. "I think we'll get the next name if the money is sent. That's what we were told."

She looked at Vail again, and her mouth relaxed into a smile the way it always did when she was about to prevail.

"It's not costing us any more than if Calculus were right here handing us the next name. . . . Then this investigation is over, Bill. We've got nothing else. . . ." After a few more seconds, she said, "Thank you," and hung up.

"It'll be wire-transferred first thing tomorrow," she said.

Vail was smiling.

"What's so funny?"

"How Langston never had a chance," he said, his voice softening, no longer ridiculing. "How so few of us do."

She tried not to blush, and then, to change the subject, she said, "So what now? You're not going to search Pollock's house?"

"If Pollock was in possession of the next name, there would have been no reason for Calculus to try to destroy the disc at the safe house."

"So if there is a string tying names together, there's only one place it can be—on the DVD," she said.

Vail turned on the monitor and pressed the Play button.

Again they watched carefully as Pollock traded

documents for money. Then the screen went to static. Wondering if Calculus had hidden something beyond the end of the video, Vail let it run for half an hour before turning it off.

Finally Kate said, "I didn't see anything."

"Me either," Vail answered slowly, his voice containing that distracted hollowness that always meant that something beyond the obvious was being considered. He got up and retrieved the disc from the player. Holding it up to the light, he checked both sides, looking for anything that didn't belong there. He sat down and rolled the disc back and forth between his fingertips. Something along the edge felt irregular, as if it had been scuffed. He went over to the desk lamp and switched it on.

"What is it?"

Searching through the desk, Vail found a fingerprint magnifier, the kind used by Bureau examiners. He held it up to the disc's edge. "There are a bunch of tiny nicks on the edge."

She got up and watched over his shoulder. "'Nicks' as in a pattern?"

"They're very slight, but uniform. Evenly spaced. There are two kinds—cuts, like the edge was slashed, and then just points, like they'd been bored straight down to make a tiny round divot. A couple dozen of them." Vail ran his finger around the disc's edge again. "They're hardly noticeable." He picked up a pencil and put the magnifier up to the DVD again. "Write this down."

Kate grabbed a pad of paper and a pen and watched as he ran the pencil point into each one to ensure he didn't miss any.

"Line, line, line, line, dot, dot, dot, dot, line, line, line, line, line, dot, dot, line, line, line, dot, dot, line, line, line, line, dot, dot, dot, dot, dot, dot, dot, dot, dot, dot, dot. Okay, let's see what we got."

Kate gave him the pad and he studied the configuration.

||||···· |||||·· |||·· |||| ···········

"Any idea what it is?" Kate asked.

"With just two characters, maybe it's a binary code, ones and zeros."

"We've got code people. Why don't we let them take a crack at it?"

"If we have to. Remember, the director's mandate: the fewer people the better. But with just two characters, it's got to be something fairly simple. Let's try to figure it out ourselves first."

Vail sat down at the desk and tore off the page. He copied it and counted the marks. "There are thirty-five characters." He took the examiner's loupe and, carefully rotating the disc, studied the edge again. "I see some spaces. It appears to be seven groups of five."

Vail rewrote the characters with the spacing:

||||· ···|| |||·· |||·· ||||· ····· ·····

He showed it to Kate.

"If this is going to identify or locate an individual, each grouping has to be either a letter or number," she said.

"And since the first and fifth groups represent

the same thing, as do the third and fourth and the last two, it's more likely they represent numbers, because there are only ten digits as opposed to twenty-six letters in the alphabet, which would show more variations and less repeating."

"Of course," she said, "seven digits. It's a telephone number. And since there apparently isn't an area code, we'll have to assume it's local—202."

"Very good, Kate. Now all we have to do is figure out the code."

Kate said, "Since the last two digits are the same, maybe they're zeros, like a business phone."

Vail stared at the patterns for a long time. Then he went to the couch and lay down, closing his eyes. Kate waited, and after a few minutes she wondered if he had fallen asleep.

"Maybe it's some sort of auditory clue," he said finally. "Could you read them to me?"

Kate sat down at the desk and read the groupings aloud. "Just keep reading them for a while," he said.

Kate read them again, and when he didn't react, she started over. Vail's eyes remained closed, his body motionless. On the fourth time through, she let her voice slip into a singsong rhythm.

Vail jerked up to a sitting position. "It's so simple. When I heard you repeating 'dot, dot, dot,' it came to me. It's not 'line, dot'—it's 'dash, dot.' It was easier and more economical to cut a perpendicular line across the edge than a dash. It's Morse code."

He was at the computer now, looking for the symbols of the code. Once they were on the screen, he said, "Write this down. Four dashes and a dot is the number nine. The first and fifth number is nine.

Three dots and two dashes is three. Three dashes and two dots is eight. And five dots is five, so the last two numbers are five."

Kate said, "It's 938-8955."

Kate picked up the phone and dialed. "This is Deputy Assistant Director Bannon. Extension 3318 Tango, please." She then enunciated the number clearly, as one does when responding to voice prompts. She repeated it. Then, after a few seconds, she smiled, wrote down the subscriber information, and hung up. "It comes back to the Russian embassy."

Vail walked over and took the number from her, pointing at the phone on the desk. "Which line has the recorder on it?"

"Line three." As he lifted the receiver to dial, she pushed the first button on the row along the bottom of the phone. He leaned toward her and turned the handset so she could listen. After four rings the voice of a middle-aged male with a noticeable Russian accent asked the caller to leave a message. Vail listened to the beep and waited until the line disconnected. "Anything?" he asked her.

"Think that was Calculus?" she asked.

"It could be. Did you hear anything out of the ordinary?"

"You mean like an anomaly?" she teased.

"Yes, Katherine, like an anomaly."

"Nope."

Vail looked back at the handwritten dots and dashes. "That's got to be it. But the message doesn't say anything."

"Maybe you need the access code to get into it—

you know, to retrieve a message like on your home machine."

"Good idea," he said. "But those can be two, three, or four digits. I suspect that with Calculus it's four digits. That's ten thousand combinations. Then no one can accidentally access it."

"Maybe it's in the phone number, the first four digits or the last four."

"Give it a try."

Kate pressed the Speakerphone button and then hit Redial. The same message played, and after the beep Vail entered the first four digits of the telephone number: 9388. There was no response. Kate disconnected the line and hit Redial again. The message replayed, and Vail tapped in 8955. Still there was no response. She said, "How about first and last four backward?"

Vail went through the procedure twice more, entering 8839 and 5598. Neither gave them access.

"Just nine thousand nine hundred and ninety-six more to go," Kate said.

Vail studied the seven digits to see if there was another logical set of four to strip out and try. Finally he turned the sheet of paper over so he couldn't see it. "It has to be something else. Something we can figure out, something so simple it's invisible."

"Like Pollock being our first fish."

Vail smiled. "You're really getting good at this. This guy isn't our first fish, but . . . ?"

"Our second," Kate said. "Zero, zero, zero, two."

Vail stood up and waved his hand at the phone ceremoniously so she could sit down and dial. Once she hit 0002, a message started to play:

"Hello, it's me—you know, Preston. I've got those infrared facial-recognition schematics you wanted, but the price has gone up. This time I want a hundred thousand dollars in cash, just for me. I've been getting the short end while taking all the chances. So this will keep it, you know, level and true." The voice chuckled briefly before he said, *"You've got my number."*

The caller hung up, and Kate started to say something, but Vail held up a finger for her to wait. After a few seconds, they heard the tones of a phone number being dialed. The line went dead. "Another phone number?" Kate said.

"Sounds like it."

"At least this time we got his first name. Preston."

"Did you notice that there was a slight emphasis on it? I would guess that's his code name. It's traditional cloak-and-dagger stuff to have one for identifying yourself to the other side."

"Then how are we supposed to figure out who this guy is? The phone number dialed at the end?"

"That was done after Preston hung up. I'm guessing Calculus punched in those numbers. Hopefully to help us identify this guy. This time he gave us the evidence first, and the puzzle is to find the name that goes with it."

"Let me get the number converted, and maybe we can go from there." She picked up the phone and called headquarters, asking for a different extension from before. "This is Deputy Assistant Director Kate Bannon. Need a readback on this touch-tone number." She pressed the phone recorder's button, and Vail listened to the number being played back. After a few seconds, Kate wrote down the number and hung up. "It reads out as 632-265-2974. Any idea where that is?"

"No."

She turned to the computer and entered the first three numbers. "There's no such area code. How can that be?"

"Maybe it's not a phone number. Maybe it's some other type of code. The first two clues were different." He stared at the ten numbers, trying various combinations. "Calculus apparently likes creating puzzles to show how smart he is."

"Or how dumb we are." Kate was also studying the numbers, looking for patterns. "Obviously we're missing something." She got a distant look in her eye, which then focused all of a sudden. "That's it! What's missing?"

Vail said, "What? What do you mean, what's missing?"

"There are no eights, ones, or zeros."

Vail looked at the line of numbers. "I still don't get it."

"Look at your cell phone."

At first he didn't understand but then examined the keys more closely. "There are no letters on the number one and zero keys. He's telling us to convert these numbers into letters from the phone." She picked up a pen, rewrote the numbers and then, underneath, the corresponding letters from the phone dial:

6	3	2	2	6	5	2	9	7	4
mno	def	abc	abc	mno	jkl	abc	wxyz	pqrs	ghi

She said, "It must be a ten-letter clue—one from each of the groups?"

"Very nice, Katie."

"Do you think it could it be a name?" she asked.

"With all the variations and spelling combinations, a name would be difficult to decode. And these clues are getting more difficult. A name seems a little too direct after all the work we had to do to get the embassy phone number and access code. Chances are it's something else."

"Like what?"

"I don't know, but let's listen to it again." He played the recorded message back. Vail struck slashes between the letters. "There are three hesitations between the groups of letters dialed. He showed her:

mno def / abc abc mno jkl / abc wxyz / pqrs ghi

"So it's a two-letter group, then four letters, a two-letter, and another two. Do you think it's four words?"

"Let's assume it is. Try the two-letter words first, since there are fewer possibilities."

Kate said, "Okay, with a letter from each group, the only possibilities for the first group are 'me' and 'of.'"

"And the third word could only be 'ax' or 'by.'"

"The last one has just one vowel, i, and that doesn't match up with p, q, r, or s."

Vail, listening intently, played the recording again. "No, that's definitely the way they're spaced. Let's try the four-letter word."

They both took a sheet of paper and wrote at the top:

abc abc mno jkl

Then they started writing down letter combinations, one from each group. After a couple of minutes, Kate said, "Have I got this right? There's only one word that you can make out of it?"

"'Bank'?" Vail asked.

"That's what I got."

Vail rewrote all the letters with the second group decoded:

mno def / BANK / abc wxyz / pqrs ghi

"'Of bank' or 'Me bank'? Neither one makes any sense," he said.

Kate said, "He's directing us to a bank. The first two letters must be an abbreviation for the name of the bank." She was up and started pulling open desk drawers until she found a phone book. Once she located bank listings, she ran her finger down the page and then stopped, smiling. "OD—Old Dominion Bank."

"I might as well go for coffee while you finish this."

Kate flashed him a brief grin of appreciation. Vail rewrote the name on another blank sheet of paper:

OLD DOMINION BANK / abc wxyz / pqrs ghi

"And what were the two words—'by' and 'ax'?— for the third word? If the bank was by something, he wouldn't need the word 'by.' In a ten-letter message, he wouldn't waste two of them on an unnecessary preposition. So it's probably another abbreviation."

Kate wrote everything on her pad of paper again. After looking at the options for only a second, she said, "How about a combination of 'by' and 'ax'— 'bx'? *Box.* It's a bank box."

Vail laughed. "How about giving us common laborers a chance?"

"And the last two are not letters—they're the original numbers from the message. The bank-box number."

"Old Dominion Bank, box 74. Very impressive, Bannon. For upper management—extraordinary."

She noticed him looking at her somehow differently, as if rediscovering something he had forgotten or never known.

"In the morning we'll have to figure out which branch has box 74," he said.

"I'll call Langston and let him know."

"How are you going to tell him we found this?"

Kate said, "He's going to have to get a court order, which means probable cause, which means we've got to tell him about the clues Calculus has left. It's urgent that we get into that box so we can identify any other spies."

"Which means he may want first crack at everything from now on."

"Yeah, Vail, like you'll let that happen."

TEN

VAIL WAS SITTING AT THE KITCHEN TABLE WITH HIS INJURED hand unwrapped, trying to cut away the stitches with a small pair of scissors when Kate came in. Without a word, she took them from him and turned his hand over so she could see the sutures better. With tiny, careful snips, she cut them loose and then pulled each one out slowly. "It looks pretty good."

He flexed his hand into a fist and then pressed the injured edge against the table. "It feels fine. What did Langston have to say last night?"

"In a very official monotone, he thanked me for the information and said he would have Kalix get to work on it. On the way over here, John called and said that after a discreet call to a contact at the Old Dominion Bank he was told that box 74 was at their Vienna, Virginia, branch. He is meeting with the prosecutor at eleven and will meet us at the bank at one o'clock unless we hear otherwise."

Vail flexed his hand again. "Did you tell him how we connected the identities?"

"No, but he's got to be starting to wonder."

"Don't forget, he's an administrator. He's used to

figuring out what to do when answers are brought to him, not where they came from."

"Let's hope it stays that way."

Vail checked his watch. "We've got to talk to those homicide detectives about Pollock. We should be done in time to get to the bank."

"What are you going to tell them about why we were looking for him?"

"We'll tell them it's a terrorist investigation. Very hush-hush."

"You know there are laws about lying to the police, even here in Washington."

"With these guys' caseloads, do you think they're going to worry about whether it was terrorism or counterintelligence? They're probably trying to figure out how to get fifteen minutes' more sleep a day."

AFTER THE HOMICIDE interviews, it was almost one o'clock by the time Vail and Kate arrived at the bank in Vienna. Bill Langston and John Kalix were already there, waiting for them in the parking lot. While she got out and went back to talk to Langston, Vail opened the trunk and loaded his briefcase with evidence gloves and envelopes. Kate came back and handed Vail the court order, which he also put in his briefcase. "Did Kalix have any trouble getting it?" he asked.

"Some. The whole thing is a little more complicated because of the secrecy angle. And you've got to admit that we are reading the tea leaves as far as what that message says. It could be an entirely different code. But I guess John finally wore them down."

"It's going to be embarrassing if we've come up with the wrong person," Vail said.

"Don't think that hasn't crossed my mind. They're going to wait in the car so it doesn't look like the FBI is overrunning the bank," she said.

Behind closed doors Kate and Vail explained to the manager about the need for confidentiality due to national security. He seemed to take the warning seriously. The bank computer revealed that an Alex Markov had rented safe-deposit box number 74 with a second name on the account of Yanko Petriv. The bank manager printed out all the account information and gave it to them.

For employment Markov had said that he was a correspondent for the Moscow newspaper *Izvestia*. For his phone number, he had given the same one Vail and Kate had called at the Russian embassy to receive the clue to Spy Number Two's identity. Vail thought it was a nice little touch by Calculus to tell them they were on the right track. Apparently there was an Ariadne thread after all.

Vail also suspected that the name Markov was another false identity that Calculus had used to open the account. The bank box was smart, a way to transfer money and documents without the risk of being seen together. At least that's how Calculus would have sold the idea to Petriv. But now it looked as if Calculus had done it to set him up. It was an easy way to plant and protect evidence that, because Petriv's name was the only true name on the box, provided irrefutable proof of treason.

Now Vail needed to determine if Yanko Petriv was the mole's real name. His employer was listed as the U.S. government. The phone number had a Virginia area code. "Can we get into the box without anyone else knowing?" Vail asked the manager.

"Sure. Just let me go tell my assistant that the boxes are closed for the next hour due to a lock malfunction. Then I'll take you down there. We're going to have to break into the box. If either of the box holders wants in, they won't be able to access it after we replace the lock. By law, the next time they try to access it, we'll have to tell them that the FBI was here and that a court order was served."

Vail wrote down his cell-phone number and handed it to the manager. "If either of them shows up, call me immediately."

"Sure."

"Okay, let's open it."

After the manager oversaw the drilling of the lock on box 74, he led Kate and Vail to a small room and left them, closing the door behind him. Kate said, "Think Markov is Calculus?"

"You recognized the phone number, too. If he is, that should mean that whatever is in this box has a lead to the next name." He lifted the lid, and they both put on evidence gloves. Inside were banded stacks of hundred-dollar bills. A quick count revealed almost forty thousand dollars. There were also a number of documents, most of which had CLASSIFIED stamped on them. Other pages included some handwritten lists, which were mostly names and phone numbers. Underneath them were two passports, one Czechoslovakian in the name of Lev

Tesar and a Hungarian one with the name Oszkar Kalman. Kate opened them both and saw that although the hair color and length were different in the photos, it was the same individual. She said, "Looks like part of Mr. Petriv's compensation package included escape plans."

"Notice anything else about this?"

"What?"

"If they were using this box as a dead drop, there should be only money in here, or documents, not both."

"Which means what?"

Vail studied the account printout the manager had given him. "Two weeks ago there was activity four days in a row. Petriv came the first day to put documents in the box. Markov—or Calculus, if you prefer—came the next day to remove them and leave money. The third day Petriv comes back and verifies the payment and moves almost ten thousand to his checking. On the fourth day, Markov makes sure some of the money is still there and puts back the documents, or probably copies of them, for us to recover. He knew that Petriv wouldn't go back into the box until another exchange was set up. That left everything there for us to find."

"Which we hope means that Calculus hid a clue to the next name in this pile of documents," Kate said. She examined the papers more closely. "According to some of the stampings on the pages, I think these might be NSA reports. I've seen similar ones. If they are, maybe this is the intelligence agent that Calculus was referring to. Maybe there were only two spies he was going to give us."

"Maybe," Vail said. "Let's pack everything up. Keep your fingers crossed that Langston won't want to see any of it."

"I'll make sure he doesn't," Kate said.

"How are you going to do that?"

She said, "We'll give him Petriv's name and phone number and tell him we need him to find out who Petriv really is and where he works. A little distraction."

"It's obvious that somewhere in your life someone taught you some bad habits."

VAIL PUSHED THE code into the off-site's alarm. As he and Kate climbed the stairs, he asked, "Did Langston seem satisfied with the division of labor on Mr. Petriv?"

"He seemed suspicious. I know he can be a little pompous, but don't take him for a fool."

"Define 'suspicious.'"

"He asked me how we came up with the bankbox information. I told him we stumbled across it. He pressed me, and when I wouldn't be more specific, I think he assumed we had done something illegal. Of course he didn't want any of that to get on his shoes. But when I told him we'd look over everything from the box and let him know if there's anything of interest, I got the feeling this is the last time we're going to get away with disguising light lifting as heavy lifting."

"Let's worry about next time next time."

After putting on a fresh pair of gloves, Kate handed a set to Vail. He spread the documents out on the table, and she asked, "How do you want to do this?"

"Let's split them into two piles. You read one while I go through the other. If we don't find anything, we'll switch."

After a few minutes, he said, "I think this document is talking about a wiretap. It refers to a target phone. Can you call and see what the number is?"

She dialed headquarters and after a short conversation hung up. "It's an importer that specializes in items from Eastern Europe."

"What government agencies specialize in wiretaps of East Europeans?"

"Which ones don't?" She smiled. "I'd better call Personnel and make sure that Petriv isn't a Bureau employee."

Vail continued looking through the papers while she made the call. After hanging up, she said, "He's not one of ours, at least not under the name Yanko Petriv. That leaves the likely suspects CIA and NSA."

"Then your initial guess of NSA is probably a good one. Just make sure you act surprised when Langston calls."

They both went back to reading the documents. After twenty more minutes, Vail pushed his last item across the table and leaned back in his chair and waited for Kate to finish.

Finally she set down her last page. "Any anomalies?"

"None. You?" he asked.

"Other than two blank sheets of paper stapled together with a couple of dates written at the bottom of one, nothing."

"Let me see them?"

She searched through the stack of pages and pulled them out.

Vail held the two papers gently between his fingers. The bottom one was a common size, about eight and a half by eleven, but the one stapled on top of it was an eight-inch square. At the base of the full-size page were the dates 12/27 and 1/6. They were written with the same careful penmanship and medium-blue ink that had been used to inscribe "Ariadne" on the water-soluble envelope. "This is what we're looking for. And these sheets have one additional *anomalous* quality: They're glossy."

"Which means?"

He turned them over a few times, finally holding each page up to the light at different angles. He took them over to the window and raised the shade. Tilting the larger page up to the bright sunlight, he shifted it around for a few more seconds. He held up the smaller one. "This is the same size as what else?"

"I don't know, what?"

He went over to the desk, set down the pages, and put the fingerprint magnifier on top of the square sheet.

"A fingerprint card," she said. "That's why he cut it to that size. So we'd recognize it."

Vail went back to the window and used the natural light to examine the smaller page with the loupe. Then he flipped it behind the full sheet and examined its surface. "I know that engineers have a reputation for not being creative, but I think Calculus is an exception. It's so simple. And so ingenious."

"*What is it?*"

Vail held up both his hands and spread the fingers apart. "What am I holding up?"

"Two hands," she said. "Ten fingers."

"Another name for fingers."

"I don't know . . . 'digits.' What?" Vail didn't answer but watched her face. All of a sudden, it dawned on her. She took the loupe from Vail's hand and locked her eye against it, running it over both sheets. When she straightened up, she smiled. "You're right, it is ingenious. He's using fingerprints as a code."

"Each finger has a number on the fingerprint card we use. The right thumb is number one, all the way to the left pinkie being number ten—or, for code purposes, zero."

After a few seconds, she again scanned the larger sheet. "The message is on this page, but we wouldn't be able to assign a number to each one without a control set of prints. The *fingerprint card*, so to speak"—she bent over the smaller page and ran the magnifier across it to confirm what she was about to say—"has a set of ten in the same order in which they'd be rolled during an arrest. From them we know what number to assign to the latents on the big page, which is the code to lead us to the next mole," Kate said. "But then what do the dates mean?"

"I don't know. First we've got to get both of these pages fumed so we can see exactly what Calculus is telling us."

Vail's cell phone rang. It was Luke Bursaw. "Steve, remember we talked about seeing if the police department had any similar patterns of missing females? Well, they do. I got copies of their reports and was wondering if you could give me a hand for a couple of hours."

"Hold on a second." Vail covered the phone. "It's Luke. He needs some help. An hour or two. It'll take that long to get those pages processed, won't it?"

"With the fuming process, yes. Go ahead, I'll get this done."

"Luke, why don't you come over here. . . . Okay, I'll see you then."

After he hung up, Kate asked, "You're going to let him see all this?" She waved a hand at all the documents and photos covering the wall.

"First of all, he is an agent. Second of all, he's Luke. I'll ask him to pretend that it isn't there, and he will."

"You're right." As though they were as fragile as archival material, Kate cautiously packed up the two sheets of paper, threading them into a clear plastic envelope before putting them into her briefcase. "I'll call you when I'm done. You and Luke aren't going to get lost, I hope. Remember, we're in a race here."

"He said a couple of hours. If it takes longer, you're going to have to yell at him."

"If there's one thing I've learned in the last six months it's who to yell at."

ELEVEN

"LUKE, DO YOURSELF A FAVOR AND IGNORE THE STUFF ON THE wall," Vail said.

Bursaw let his eyes briefly scan the documents and said, "You always did thrive on chaos." He took out a sheaf of papers. "These are homicide reports on three women who were killed in the last six months."

"Give me a few minutes to read them." The ability to ignore agency boilerplate was a necessary skill for anyone in law enforcement, and Vail had regained his in the few days of being back to reading Bureau reports. "I think there's some coffee."

"I could use a couple of cups." Bursaw got up and started toward the kitchen. "What is this place?"

"Across the street is the old Russian embassy. You know, before they built the new one up on Tunlaw Road."

"Then this was an observation post?"

"Tough duty, huh?"

"You want some coffee?" Bursaw called over his shoulder as he entered the kitchen.

"No!" Vail yelled after him. "All three of these women were prostitutes."

Bursaw came back in with a cup in his hand. "I

know that Sundra doesn't exactly fit into the victimology pattern of these women, but she disappeared during the same six-month period as they did," Bursaw said. "Does that mean you don't think they're related to her disappearance?"

"Not necessarily. If it is the same guy, she could have known him or unwittingly presented him with an opportunity. His MO is to take women in very low-risk situations. Prostitutes have to go with him. It's unlikely that he would try something risky like grabbing Sundra anywhere she would have a chance to resist."

"If you're suggesting it might be someone who knew her, I've already interviewed everyone I could find, from names in her address book to people my cousin knew, including casual acquaintances like the UPS guy or anyone else she might know without really knowing. So far nothing."

"Then I'd say this is your best bet right now."

Bursaw took a sip of his coffee. "Come on, Steve." He waved at the wall. "I can see you've got a lot going on, but I need you to fire up that twisted brain of yours in Sundra's direction."

"Give me a few minutes to think about it." Vail walked into the kitchen and poured himself a cup of coffee. When he came back, he said, "You told me that Sundra had a new computer. Was it taken into evidence?"

"Yes. I've already gone through it. There really wasn't much on it."

"Take it to the lab and have them go through it. I read about a new forensics technique called Volume Shadow Copy. It allows them to reconstruct a computer's hard drive on any given day. Start with the day she disappeared and then each day before that to see if anything was purged. If it was, get a copy of it, and we'll take a look at it."

Bursaw made a note. "Volume Shadow Copy. Okay."

"What about her work computer?" Vail asked.

"I know they've downloaded everything off it from the server and then dry-cleaned it so no one else could get access to it. As far as I know, nothing was found."

"Again, get a printout, and we can take a look at it. Maybe the two of them together will tell us something that each alone wouldn't."

"Actually, that's not a bad lead. Although it was strictly against Bureau policy, she was known to copy files onto her personal computer and work on cases at home. I'll get on it."

"In the meantime we should look into the three dead prostitutes. I assume you're checking to see if there are any women out there who've gotten away from this guy."

"As we learned in Detroit, a surviving victim is still the best way to find out who's killing hookers. I'm having them put together a list of serious assaults on ladies of the evening in that general area right now."

"All you need is one."

Bursaw drained his cup. "Thanks, Steve. So, you staying here? I saw the cots in the room off the kitchen."

"Free room and board. Life is good."

"I thought maybe you were staying at Kate's."

"At the moment it's all business."

"Moments pass."

"Evidently you don't know Kate as well as you think you do."

VAIL WAS JUST dozing off on the couch when Kate called. "I've got the pages fumed. Are we going to need someone to figure out which finger is which?"

"How clear are they?"

"As clean as if they'd been inked," Kate said.

"Then I can do it."

"I'm on my way."

"HI," KATE SAID as soon as she came through the door. "How'd it go with Luke?"

"More tilting at windmills than finding lost women, I'm afraid."

"So you're done with it now?"

He looked at her, and she knew his answer before he said anything. "Probably not. Sorry." He pulled on a fresh pair of gloves. "Let's see what we've got."

Amused, Kate said, "So you came here to go to a cocktail party, and now you're working a third case. Sounds like somebody needs to learn how to say no."

He gave her a sarcastic grin. "Should I decide to get some instruction, I know an expert who delivers the word with extreme malice."

"I'm willing to bet you know several." Carefully, she pulled out the sheets of paper, which now had a purple cast to them.

He took the fingerprint loupe and said, "On the

code page, there are three prints on each line and three lines, nine impressions. So we're going to get nine numbers out of this. With any luck they won't represent something else. Start thinking about what has nine numbers and can identify a person."

"Actually, I was thinking about it on the way here. There's only one that comes to mind—a Social Security number."

"Sounds reasonable." Vail examined the top row of prints. He compared it to the prints from the "fingerprint card." "The first one is the left ring finger, so number nine." Kate wrote it down. He examined the second latent. "The left index finger—seven." He continued, line by line, until all nine latents had been decoded. "Okay, what have we got?"

She handed Vail the pad of paper with the nine numbers written on it. She had placed dashes after the third and fifth, making it read like a Social Security number. He handed it back. "How can we find out who it belongs to?"

She went over and sat down at the computer. "Let me see if they have an Accurint program on here." After logging on to the Internet and clicking the mouse a couple of times, she said, "Yes." She signed in to the program with her password and then typed in the nine digits. After a few seconds, a secondary screen popped up. "James Dellasanti. Currently residing just outside Wheaton, Maryland."

"Can it tell us where he works?"

"Sometimes, but it's a different query." She punched a few more keys, and the screen changed. "No, not this time. Let me check and see if we did a background investigation for his clearance." She switched into a Bureau program and queried the name. "Well, the good news is, he doesn't work for the FBI or any agency we do the backgrounds for." When Vail didn't say anything, she said, "We could give this to Langston, too. Let him do the cut-and-paste stuff."

"We can't. We don't have any evidence against this Dellasanti. With the others we have a DVD and then stolen documents with money in a bank box. Here we have nothing but a set of numbers that we're not even sure is a Social Security number. And where's the link to the next mole, if there is one? There's got to be more to this."

"Then it has to be the dates." She looked at the page. "December twenty-seventh and January sixth."

"Maybe, but what do they mean?"

"One date has passed, and the other's coming up in two days."

Thinking about what she'd said, Vail walked over to the wall covered with the maps and reports documenting Calculus's travels. "Can you get into the spy satellite again?"

Kate started tapping the keys and after a minute said, "We're up."

"Okay, let me read you his coordinates from December twenty-seven. Just the places he stopped for more than five minutes."

After she wrote the numbers down, he moved behind her and watched as she manipulated the mouse until the coordinates were in the small windows on the screen. She zoomed in. "The first one is the Russian embassy compound."

"That's to be expected. Try the next one."

She entered it and then zoomed down to ground level. "That's a fairly busy intersection with a McDonald's right there."

Vail went back to the wall. "He was there about twenty minutes and it was approximately eleven thirty. So it was probably a Big Mac lunch. Next one."

After locating the third coordinate and zooming down to it, she said, "It's a public park in Maryland."

"That's it!"

"That's what?"

"That's what January six is. A dead-drop date."

"How do you know that?"

"It's well documented that the Russians love parks for exchanging money and information. And it's also well known that they hate changing a procedure when they find one that works." Vail went back up to the wall and rechecked the entry. "He was there eighteen minutes. Calculus was picking up the information from Dellasanti, who evidently is supposed to go back there on the sixth and retrieve his payment."

"Don't you think that's a lot of supposition based on a couple of written dates?"

"You're right." He turned back to the wall and searched Calculus's movements again. "Here," he said, pointing at a document, "the following day he was at the same coordinates for twelve minutes."

"He was putting the documents back."

"Probably copies. He would have to turn in the originals because his bosses would have to see them to okay the payment."

Kate said, "So the day after, he put the copies there with the payment? For us to catch Dellasanti with?"

Vail was tracking Calculus's movements again. "He never went back there after that, so it has to be. And by writing down the second date, he's telling us exactly when he'll pick up the package."

"And then Calculus told him the money wouldn't be there until January sixth. This time the evidence is actually catching him in the act," she said. "What better proof?"

"Exactly," Vail said. "Can you walk the camera around a little?"

"Sure. What are you looking for?"

"Someplace for the drop. Someplace you could hide a package of documents or money and not have it bothered by people or weather. That's why parks are so popular for this kind of thing. Especially in the winter."

Kate's eyes were locked on the screen as she virtually strolled through the park. "Here's something close by, maybe twenty yards away—a footbridge."

Vail came around the computer and stared at the monitor. "Perfect," he said, then pointed. "See underneath the end there? You could easily hide a good-size package." Vail went back to the wall to check the coordinates of the bridge. "Okay, he was there for about three minutes, and then he walked around a little, stopping here and there for a minute or two. Probably to look less conspicuous."

"But the bridge, that's where you figure he left the package."

"That'd be my guess."

"Can I call Langston now?"

"Okay, but tell him not to send anyone to the dead drop. We have to assume if Calculus told the Russians everything, they could be watching it. If they spot our people, there's probably a good chance that Dellasanti will be killed."

Kate asked, "If the Russians do have the Calculus list, why aren't they just taking all of them out instead of waiting to see if we're going to arrest them?"

"They're probably still productive sources, and good ones are not easy to come by. Also, should it ever surface in the future that the Russians are killing their moles, recruiting new ones would be impossible."

"I'd better quit putting off calling Langston. Even though this should be good news, that we've found another one, I've got a feeling he isn't going to like it. We're figuring out who these people are faster than we can arrest them."

"Actually, it only seems a little complicated at this point. Spy Number One, Charles Pollock, is dead. Spy Number Two, Yanko Petriv, with a little luck is in the process of being fully identified for arrest, and Number Three, James Dellasanti, will be caught in the act in two days in Maryland. As you reminded me earlier today, speed is what's important here. It doesn't matter if everyone's happy about it, or if it's legal enough to put in their memoirs. The Russians already have the list and apparently are willing to kill these people to keep them out of our hands. And don't forget the 'big fish.' That's the real prize we're trying to beat them to."

"That all sounds nice, but in case you haven't noticed, very little of this has gone as planned. What if
something happens, like Dellasanti deciding to pick
up whatever's at the drop before the sixth?"

"He's probably been told that the money won't
be there until January sixth. And spies hate going
to the dead drop—it's when they're most exposed. If
Calculus put the documents back like he did in the
bank box—and according to that tracking phone, it
looks as if he did—we'll have him along with the evidence and money all in one nice neat little package.
We just have to make sure that you and I get our
hands on whatever documents might be there before
anyone else does. Especially if Dellasanti isn't the
'big fish.' I don't want to lose control until we figure
out who that is. If Langston gets the idea in his head
that he can take over, he'll have to play by the rules,
and I think if this case has proved anything, it's that
this isn't going to get solved that way."

"As uncomfortable as I am with deceiving him, I
guess you're right." Kate looked at her watch. "I des-
perately need to catch up on my other job's paperwork. And I'd better let Langston know about this
upcoming drop by no later than tomorrow morning.
We'll need to get surveillance on it ahead of time."

"Just make sure he's going to let us handle that
package."

"I'll do my best. In the meantime, if Langston
has Petriv identified, we should be able to round
him up tomorrow. And then, with a little luck, Dellasanti the next day," Kate said. "This whole thing
wouldn't seem nearly as daunting if we knew how
many names were left."

"I told you before, spies love mind games. Answers are better protected if they're surrounded by confusion."

Kate slipped her coat on. "What are you going to do with the night off?"

"I hadn't thought about it. Maybe have dinner with Luke."

"By 'dinner' you mean work on his missing analyst."

Vail smiled. "I wouldn't be surprised if it came up."

TWELVE

VAIL AND BURSAW SAT IN THE FRONT SEAT OF THE WFO agent's car. Between them were take-out orders of hamburgers and fries. They were in southeast D.C. watching a street corner that was busy with prostitutes flagging down cars. "Is this what passes for dinner theater in Washington?" Vail asked.

"I thought it would be nostalgic for you. You probably haven't talked to a hooker since you were run out of Detroit."

"For the record, I wasn't run out—I walked. Let me see her picture again."

Bursaw handed him the mug shot of Denise Washington. Her hair was matted, and her skin was washed out and blemished by continual drug abuse. Vail handed it back. "I could be wrong, but didn't you bring her to the Christmas party one year in Detroit?"

"That's right. It was the year you brought that 'exotic dancer' with the Adam's apple."

"Fool me once . . ."

Bursaw laughed. "I wish she'd show up. It's getting to be the drive-by-shooting hour, and I'm already spending way too much time in court."

They continued eating for the next few minutes.

"Maybe we should deputize one of these girls. Put her on the payroll, and she could give you a call when the fair Denise shows up."

"What are the chances of a hooker calling me?"

"A good-looking African-American like yourself, plus twenty dollars? Don't sell yourself short." Vail straightened up. "That's her there, isn't it?"

Bursaw took a closer look at the young woman getting out of a pickup truck. "Now, see, Vail, that's why I wanted you here. Not because you're any kind of agent, but because you are the world's luckiest white man." Pulling away from the curb, Bursaw drove for a half block before making a U-turn. He coasted back to where the young woman stood and stopped in front of her. He rolled down the window and leaned across Vail. "Denise!"

She looked at the two men who were obviously law enforcement and shook her head disgustedly. "I ain't doing nothing," she protested.

"We're not here for that. Get in the backseat."

"I didn't do nothing." He flipped open his credentials, and she said, "FBI? I sure as hell didn't do nothing *that* bad."

"I'm here about the man who attacked you."

The other girls were starting to move away from the corner. Denise smiled. "Well, what kept you boys?" She strutted comically for the other girls, as if she were getting into a limousine. Once the door was closed, she said, "I hope you're here to tell me that you caught that freak."

Bursaw turned around in his seat and said, "I just found out about it today. But I'm making it a priority. Did you know him?"

"Never saw him before."

"Ever date him?"

"Not me, but some of the other girls told me they did."

Bursaw handed her the photographs of the three prostitutes that had been murdered. "Any of these girls?"

She shuffled past the first two, but the third girl caused a reaction. "You think he's the one who killed Darlene?"

"That's what we'd like to ask him. Tell me about what happened with you."

"You sure we're cool?"

"This is what it is, Denise. Nothing else."

"Okay, but if it ain't, this is entrapment."

"I'll consider myself warned," Bursaw said.

"I guess it was two or three months ago. He pulls up, and I ask him what he wants. He agrees to the money, and I get in. He had this old van, the kind with no windows. He drives for a couple of blocks. I could tell he knew where he was going. Some dead-end street, just factories and stuff. I tell him I need the money up front. He gives me a twenty, and we start to get busy. All of a sudden, he's got this screwdriver pressed to my neck and tells me to get in the back. I hesitate, and he jabs it into my skin." She lifted her head. "I still got a scar." Both agents inspected the rectangular mark that the tip of a screwdriver would leave. "So I get in the back. Once I'm there, I see he's got ropes tied to the inside braces on the walls, four of them. I've been doing this long enough to know I was in trouble. He sets down the screwdriver so he can use both his hands to tie me. I waited until he was just about to tighten the first knot, and then I picked up the screwdriver and stabbed him with it. I must have hit him pretty good, because he fell back yelling in pain. Then I jumped out and ran as fast as I could."

"Have you seen him since?"

"I haven't."

"Did you talk to the other girls about him?"

"Sure. We're always warning each other. But if it's slow out here, you know, you're not as careful."

"According to the report you filed, it happened after Darlene was killed."

"That sounds about right. You think it was this freak?"

"She was tortured, and both ankles and wrists had rope burns on them."

"Jesus Almighty. It's got to be him, then."

"Tell me about the van—what color, make, model, whatever you can."

"All I remember is it was old, maybe white, with some big rust spots on it. I couldn't tell you what kind. There was fast-food wrappers and a bunch of other garbage in the back, like he never cleaned it."

"Describe him."

"Black, maybe in his thirties. Medium build. Had his head shaved. Never saw him standing up, so I don't know how tall he was, but probably average."

"Where did you stab him?" Vail asked.

"You know, I just lashed out. I think it was in the chest."

"Think you got any depth?"

"It felt like it. And the way he fell back, I'm pretty sure I did."

Bursaw took out a dozen business cards and handed them to her. "Give these to the other girls. Anybody sees him, call me twenty-four hours a day. Let them know there's a decent chance that one of them could be next. The best thing we can get is a license plate. It's worth some money."

"If this's the fool who did Darlene that way, it'd be an insult to her to take money."

She got out of the car and leaned back in the window. "You really FBI?" she asked Bursaw. Then she got a mischievous grin on her face. "Ain't this the part where you're supposed to give me the lecture about getting out of the life?"

"Since you didn't pay any attention to the guy with the screwdriver, why would I bother?"

She laughed a single syllable and backed away from the car. "I'm going to call you, Mr. FBI. One way or the other."

As Bursaw pulled away from the curb, Vail said, "Looks like somebody's got a date for this year's Christmas party."

AT A FEW minutes before nine the next morning, Vail walked into the assistant director's office. He had received a call from John Kalix that a meeting had been scheduled to plan Yanko Petriv's arrest. Kate was sitting at a small conference table, along with Kalix and the three unit and section chiefs Vail had been introduced to at the off-site on New Year's Day. He sat down next to her. "Where's the boss man?" he asked.

Kalix said, "He's at the Department of Justice, getting authorization for Petriv's arrest."

"Have you found out where he works?"

Kalix said, "NSA. He was born in Bulgaria, and currently he's a Bulgarian and Czech interpreter for them. Those lists of handwritten phone numbers you found in the safe-deposit box are some of the phones they're up on. Bill talked to his counterpart over there last night and let them know what we've found. They called back this morning and said they haven't gotten anything off those wires in over two months. Previously they'd been fairly productive."

The door opened, and Bill Langston walked in with another man, someone Vail hadn't seen before, but he had an idea who it was. "Everyone, this is Lance Wimert from OPR."

Vail leaned over to Kate. "I wonder who he could be here to see."

Langston continued, "We're green-lighted to detain Mr. Petriv."

"By 'detain' you mean arrest, right?" Kate asked.

"I mean *detain*, as in hold with extremely slow due process. Justice has consented to this approach because of the possibility of others on the list fleeing. Once we grab him, our ten-day clock will start ticking. I've talked to NSA and explained the evidence to them. They're setting up Petriv at work for us. He'll be called away from his desk, and we will casually escort him out. I should be getting a call any minute to let us know that everything is set."

Vail said to Kate, "Did you tell him about Dellasanti?"

"Yes, she called me last night," the assistant director said. "So I called the director. Mark, you're handling that."

The unit chief, Mark Brogdon, straightened up. "I have an entire surveillance squad ready to go. They'll be in the park late tonight and look for some good spots to get an eyeball on the bridge. They don't know any of the specifics, except that they'll be covering a potential dead drop."

Kate looked at Vail and, as if anticipating what he was going to ask, said, "If Dellasanti does pick up the package, Bill wants us to take custody of it and see if we can find the next link."

Langston said, "I have to give it to you, Steve, the two of you figuring out that fingerprint code. Very slick. Apparently Calculus left clues each time so we could figure out the next name. Am I correct?"

Kate had been right about Langston's being nobody's fool. He had figured out the connection between the moles without the advantage of the Ariadne inscription. "He has so far."

"Knowing your disdain for management, it's not that hard to figure out why you didn't tell anyone about it." He looked at Kate. "At least not any of my people."

"If you check my old performance ratings," Vail said, "you'll see that 'doesn't work well with others' was one of my more consistent character flaws."

Langston chuckled. "I could see where you'd be a nightmare to manage, but you do get results. It's unfortunate you won't be able to go with us today to detain Mr. Petriv."

Vail looked at the agent from OPR and then at Kate. "Me and Lance going to spend a little time together?"

"There are some legitimate concerns about Pollock's death that need to be answered immediately," Langston said.

"Like what?"

"The syringe that was recovered from the crime scene had one set of prints on it—yours. Do you know what was in it? Temazepam. Do you know what that is?"

"A depressant."

"Yes, it is, but do you know what intelligence agencies have been rumored to use it for? Truth serum. Pollock looked like he'd been tortured and then given a truth drug. By us. The Russians don't use it. They have their own proprietary blend, something called SP-17, according to a defector. So that leaves us holding the temazepam bag. Do you see a pattern here? There can be no explanation that doesn't sound like we're covering something up. Especially with you being—no pun intended—a *contract* employee."

"There was a deputy assistant director with me. Do you think she was involved in torture?"

"I don't think either one of you was," Langston said. "This is a potentially catastrophic public-relations problem that has to be defused immediately. OPR spends a lot more time clearing our employees than having them prosecuted. And Kate will be interviewed, too, once your statement has been taken and analyzed. OPR has decided to interview you first because of your constant threat to just quit and jump on a plane to Chicago."

Vail laughed and then looked at Kate. She looked away. So she knew that this was coming, he thought.

The only reason he'd accepted the director's offer was the hope of reinstating Kate's reputation, which had been momentarily tarnished by the ridiculous assumption that she'd attempted suicide. He got up and walked to the door. He turned and looked at Kate and the men around her. Evidently she had been returned to a full-share member of the team. For whatever that was worth. Would her career always come between them? He turned back to Langston. "Nicely done, Bill."

"I had nothing to do with this. You're the one who went sneaking off on your own and wound up in the middle of this mess."

"That fingerprint exam on the syringe and the blood chemistry that found the temazepam—you didn't have that expedited?"

Langston's usual stoic expression twisted into a knot of anger fueled by the embarrassment of being caught in a lie. Just then his phone rang. He took his time going to his desk to compose himself. "Bill Langston." As he listened, he sat down and pulled a pen out of a desk holder. "I see. . . . Yes, I do, but give it to me anyhow." He wrote something down and hung up. "Petriv didn't show up for work today, and he didn't call in," he announced to everyone, and then looked at Vail.

Vail glanced back at him and then at Kate. Still she didn't meet his eyes. Apparently he'd been in denial about her truly wanting to end their relationship. But was he reading this correctly, or was he just feeling contempt for everything because he was being so artfully removed from the case? Something this confusing usually just made him mad, but instead he was feeling defiant, defiance being his oldest and most reliable ally. "Good luck."

Kate knew what that meant. Everybody in the world was on his own. Especially Steve Vail. She had seen something deep in his eyes, something only she recognized—revenge. It was perhaps his only selfish indulgence. He would find some way to involve himself in the case and succeed when everyone else failed. And then he would walk away, his final measure of contempt for the FBI and those who thought they ran it.

After Vail and the OPR agent left, Langston tore the page off the notepad. "I've got his home address. Let's go."

THIRTEEN

IT WAS IN THE MIDDLE OF THE AFTERNOON WHEN VAIL FIN-
ished with OPR. The two agents who interviewed him had never been involved in a murder
investigation before and peppered him with clumsy
questions and half-thought-out accusations in an attempt to force inconsistencies in his story. He suspected that this was also part of Langston's delaying
process. When they started asking the same questions for the third time, Vail said, "You do realize
that you have no jurisdiction in a murder case? The
only authority you have over me is as an employee,
which in a couple of days you'll have to be a Chicago
building inspector to maintain. But you can now tell
Langston that you did your job and kept me from
being involved in what he's doing. Congratulations,
I'm sure it won't be long before you'll be promoted
to assistant bosses in the field, where you'll be able
to obstruct more than one agent at a time." He got
up and walked out.

Vail checked his watch and, reluctantly, turned
on his cell phone. He was hoping Kate had called,
but she hadn't. He took a moment to scold himself
for not being able to let go of her apparent siding
with Langston. There was one message, though. It

was from the manager at the Old Dominion Bank where they had broken into Yanko Petriv's safe-deposit box.

Vail called him back. "Yes, Agent Vail, Mr. Petriv called this morning and spoke with one of the assistant managers. I had flagged his file, so when she saw it, she came to me."

"I appreciate it."

"He told her that he wanted his accounts transferred to a bank in New York and was in the process of doing the paperwork with them. In the meantime he wanted his ATM limit upped. She told him he was already at the max, four hundred dollars, and bank policy wouldn't allow it to be increased. She said he was not happy."

"Did she tell him about his safe-deposit box being opened?"

"I'm the only one here who knows about that, so she couldn't have."

"Can you take a look at his account right now?" Vail asked.

"Give me two seconds." Vail's thoughts again drifted to Kate while he waited. "Yes, I've got it up now."

"Did he make any ATM withdrawals yesterday or today?"

"Ah, let's see. Yes, this morning. Looks like just before he called us. Four hundred dollars."

"Where at?"

"At one of our branches in Arlington. In fact, I don't live far from there. It's right next to the old Adams Hotel."

"Thanks for your help," Vail said, and hung up.

He drove back to the off-site and ran upstairs to the workroom. He leafed through some of his notes until he found what he was looking for. Back in the car, he headed to the Adams Hotel.

THE TWO MEN sat parked in the SUV, which was positioned anonymously among the rows of cars at the strip mall, watching the entrance to the Adams Hotel. Vail pulled up and turned his car over to the valet. The SUV's driver dialed his cell phone, calling the man who had set the fire at the historic building, trying to kill Vail and Kate. "He just arrived."

"He's alone?"

"Get things ready there," the driver said.

"I thought the woman was our target."

Instead of answering, the driver hung up.

The big passenger with the Russian accent said, "We'll wait until he leaves to make sure he's heading in the right direction."

THE ADAMS HOTEL was one of those grand old wooden structures that looked as though Civil War generals had stayed there. It almost seemed out of place with the modern Old Dominion Bank on one side and the tall, gleaming gold-glass office building on the other. The desk clerk was an older man with a thin, waxy mustache who looked like someone out of a 1940s black-and-white movie. "May I help you?"

Vail flashed his credentials and leaned closer in

confidence. "I'm looking for a fugitive. His name is Yanko Petriv. I'd like to know if he's staying here. P-E-T-R-I-V."

The clerk studied Vail's face briefly and then, apparently satisfied, tapped a couple of keys on his desktop computer. "I'm sorry, no."

Vail took a slip of paper out of his jacket pocket. "How about Lev Tesar?" Vail spelled the last name. When the bank manager told him during the call about the hotel's being next door, Vail thought it was a possibility that Petriv might be staying there. Since Petriv had false passports, Vail reasoned that the Russians would have provided him with other corroborating identification that, since it wasn't in the safe-deposit box, might have been kept in a more immediately accessible place.

"No, sir, he's not one of our guests either."

"Last one, how about Oszkar Kalman? With a *K*."

The clerk tapped in the name. "Yes. He was."

"*Was?*"

"Yes, he checked out around noon today."

"Did he make any phone calls?"

"Ahhhh, yes, one." The clerk read the number, and Vail recognized it as the call to the Old Dominion Bank that morning.

"What address did he give you?"

The clerk looked around and then said, "I don't know if I'm allowed to provide that information without a subpoena or some other legal order." He then half turned the monitor toward Vail and gave him a tacit glance. "I have to go do something. I'll return in a couple of minutes."

"Thanks for your help," Vail called after him as he disappeared through a doorway behind the desk. He swung the monitor enough so he could read it and copied down the address Oszkar Kalman had used. It was in Oakton, Virginia.

The drive took longer than Vail had predicted, and it was almost five o'clock by the time he got to Oakton. The traffic was heavy, and two separate accidents hadn't helped. The address turned out to be an old, weathered, two-story home with a large attached garage that looked like it could have been a separate barn at one time. In an attempt to update the structure, a breezeway had been built connecting the house and garage. The nearest neighbors were a half mile in either direction. Due to some intermittent stands of pine trees, Vail was able to find a place to park seventy-five yards away that was ideal for watching the house. The thick wooden sliding doors to the garage were open a few inches, and he tried to see if he could spot any vehicles inside. He took the binoculars from under the seat and peered through them, but dusk had started to take over and the winter light was fading.

Vail thought he saw some movement in a second-floor window, but by the time he swung the binoculars toward it, there was nothing he could see. He lowered the glasses but continued to watch the second floor. A few seconds later, in the same window, he saw definite movement. As dark as it was getting, that there were no lights on meant that someone was trying not to be detected.

Vail put the car in gear and started toward the

house. As it got closer, he let it glide to a stop fifty yards in front of the garage.

Suddenly a three-round volley was fired from the second floor, at least two of the slugs slamming into the front of his car. He dove out of it and took cover behind the vehicle. After a minute or so, he peeked over the trunk, looking for any further movement inside the house.

"I thought the bumper sticker said that Virginia was for lovers," he muttered to himself.

Two more rounds were fired at him, this time from the first floor. "Evidently it's gun lovers."

He stood up and fired a burst into the first-floor window. Almost immediately he was fired at again, this time from the breezeway. He suspected that whoever was shooting at him was working his way to the garage, probably trying to get to his car. Vail shifted his angle behind the car to the garage and put his point of aim at the six-inch opening between the two heavy doors, then waited.

Almost too predictably, a three-round fusillade came from the narrow black opening between the garage doors. Vail opened fire, letting his Glock come back down level before pulling the trigger each time, as though he sensed that his rounds were finding their mark. Maybe it was the tiny after-echo that couldn't have been anything but lead slamming into tissue. He rolled back into a safe position on the car's trunk, dropped an empty magazine, and shoved in a fresh one.

Raising his head for a few seconds, he tried to draw more fire. When none came, he assumed a two-handed grip on his gun and started cautiously toward the garage. Every few feet he took a step to the right or the left so he wouldn't be a constant target. When he got to within ten feet of the garage, another eruption of gunfire came from the opening.

Vail went into a deep defensive crouch and fired at least ten rounds in the direction of the garage while he maneuvered quickly to his left and ran to the door on that side, flattening himself against it. Now the gunman would have to actually stick his weapon outside the opening to get a shot at him. He was about to take hold of the left edge of the door and slide it completely open, all the time ready to shoot anyone who stepped out, when the sound of an engine roared inside the garage. He leaped to the opening and pulled the door open.

Tied to the front of a car, spread-eagled and gagged, was Yanko Petriv, the NSA translator. At least a half dozen of Vail's rounds having found his chest and stomach.

Out of the rear of the garage, which had identical sliding doors, a blue sedan screamed away and down a back road.

Vail ran around to the other side of the garage, trying to get a shot at the car, but with its lights off it disappeared behind a stand of evergreens and into the winter night.

Vail holstered his weapon and returned to the body. Placing an index finger on Petriv's carotid artery out of habit, he withdrew it almost immediately.

He realized now that they'd had Petriv use this address so Vail would be led here. And then started the running gun battle so he'd fire blindly into the garage. Of course it wasn't his fault, and yet he couldn't help but wonder if they'd staked Petriv out like that because they knew the way Vail went after things.

FOURTEEN

VAIL HAD GOTTEN IN ABOUT FOUR HOURS EARLIER, AFTER A long session with the Oakton police. He'd called them to the scene and, as soon as they arrived, had explained that he was the one who'd shot Petriv. As he walked them through the shoot-out, they found cartridges at every location where Vail said he'd received fire. The bullet holes in his car matched the caliber of the casings recovered. When asked who the victim was, Vail said that Petriv had been a person of interest in a Bureau investigation, a man he was trying to locate, and that he had finally found him at this house.

The detective asked him more than once to clarify "person of interest," to which he answered that it was a classified matter. Finally Vail had them call Kate at home and have her verify that it was a sensitive investigation. She asked to speak to the chief and eventually convinced him that it was a matter of national security and that as soon as it was resolved, he would receive full details. After a few more hours of interviews by different combinations of officers, detectives, and even the chief, Vail was allowed to leave.

Vail woke up abruptly, thinking he'd heard Kate

calling his name. "Steve, we're coming up." It was her. He jumped out of bed and pulled on a robe.

Vail went to the top of the stairs and was surprised to see Langston and Kalix with her. "I wonder what this could be about," Vail said to himself quietly. And then, "Great, now I'm being sarcastic to myself."

They all went into the workroom, and Langston immediately noticed the wall where all the photos and documents were displayed. For a moment he tried to comprehend how they had translated into the identification of three spies, but he didn't want Vail to think he was there to admire his work.

Vail said, "Anyone want coffee?" and started for the kitchen.

Langston finally sat down on the sofa and called in to Vail, "I've briefed the director about last night, and of course he knew about the murder of Charles Pollock. Needless to say, he's not happy. Two suspected spies, both dead. Both, it appears, were tortured and killed. Both times you're right in the middle of it."

Vail came out of the kitchen. "That shows you how misguided I am. I would think it was a good thing for the Bureau to be right in the middle of things."

"And you had to go out there by yourself to do this. Was that to embarrass me?"

"I went by myself so your rules wouldn't get in the way. Embarrassing you was just a bonus."

"Apparently you don't understand what a potential nightmare this could be if the media gets hold of it."

"That's exactly why the Russians did it," Kate offered.

Langston said, "I'm well aware of that, but who's going to believe us?"

Vail sat down in a chair. Kalix, in an attempt to reduce the tension, said, "I think the big question here is why would the Russians kill Pollock and Petriv? That's never been their style."

Kate said, "Maybe this is a small group of loose Russian cannons inside the SVR who are trying too hard to please their superiors—or, more likely, not wind up in gulags. When you have an asset exposed, it makes you look incompetent. You've got to hand it to them. They've found a way to turn their losing a spy into a black eye for the Bureau."

"That's a reasonable explanation, Kate," Langston said. "Do you or Steve have any idea how they knew we were onto Petriv?"

Vail said, "The only thing I can think of is Calculus giving up his list. If he did, the Russians would be watching those individuals. Maybe even asking them that if anything unusual happens to contact the embassy immediately. In Pollock's case they probably knew we were coming because of the break-in at the safe house and the missing DVD. With Petriv, he knew we were onto the bank because he tried to get more money through the ATM when he had much more in his safe-deposit box. Somehow he knew we had been to the bank and probably assumed we were staking it out. Or maybe someone let the cat out of the bag at NSA after you contacted them the day before. You know how there are no secrets inside the Bureau. You have to assume NSA has the same rumor mill. And since we found the false passports, the Russians had probably told him that they would get him out of the country should anything happen. If so, his next step would be to call his handler."

"That also makes sense. All the more reason to bring Dellasanti in as soon as possible," Langston said. "So let's get focused on today. Surveillance is already on the drop at the park. There's no activity yet. We've also got two crews on Dellasanti—who, by the way, works for the State Department."

"I assume we're going to arrest him as soon as he makes the pickup," Kate said.

"Uh . . ." Langston glanced at Vail.

She, too, looked over at Vail, who had a small, cynical grin on his face.

"What the assistant director doesn't want to tell you," he said, "is that I will not be making the trip to Maryland."

"Since you figured that out, Steve, I assume you understand why," Langston said.

"I'm oh for two bringing in spies alive, and because I'm a very temporary employee, someone might interpret those deaths as the reason I was brought into this case."

"Is that true?" Kate asked Langston.

"Obviously it makes enough sense that he figured it out."

"You do realize that we've gotten this far only because of Steve," she said.

"It's okay, Kate," Vail told her. "They're right. The Russians are playing this beautifully." He turned to Langston. "Maybe it's time for me to bow out permanently."

Langston said, "Absolutely not. The director was vehement about that. No, we just want some space between you and Dellasanti. And I think you understand that ultimately, by using this tack, you'll be protecting yourself."

"Yes, that's always been my favorite thing about the Bureau, how they look out for me," Vail said.

Langston's cell phone rang. "Assistant Director Langston." He listened for a moment and then hung up. "Dellasanti has just left his home. It looks like he's heading to work."

"Is the drop on his way?" Kate asked.

"No. Not in the direction he's heading. We've got time."

Vail stood up. After his call to Kate in the middle of the night and her efforts to get him cleared of the Petriv shooting, he felt that maybe he had judged her too quickly after he was excluded from the Petriv case. There was one way to find out where she really stood. "It appears I've got the day off. Since Kate hasn't knifed or shot anyone, I assume she's going with you."

"Yes."

Vail stared at her for a second too long, hoping it would remind her of their deal that he was supposed to get a first look at the documents from the impending dead drop. "Don't forget you promised to call that guy Ariadne," he said to her.

VAIL SAT ALONGSIDE Luke Bursaw's desk, scanning the mountain of information printed out from the missing analyst's work computer. "I'm never using a computer again. There isn't a keystroke that isn't permanently recorded."

"It would take a year to analyze all this," Bursaw said.

"What about her personal laptop?" Vail asked.

"That—what did you call it?—Shadow Copy stuff? They're working on it now."

"Good. Have you heard anything from your girlfriend Denise?"

"Nothing. You know the attention span of a hooker. It's only about as long as their tricks."

"All this wheel spinning is making me hungry. How about I let you buy me some lunch."

"The way you eat, it'd be cheaper for me to get you a hooker."

"Sounds like somebody's been getting the law-enforcement discount."

BURSAW AND VAIL sat in a booth eating corned beef sandwiches at a deli two blocks from the Washington Field Office. "Does your supervisor know you're putting all this time in looking for Sundra?"

"We're all a little surprised when he actually finds his way to the office every day. The word is he's got much greater ambitions. All indications are that he's saving himself so when he gets back to headquarters he can screw up cases Bureau-wide."

"So what do you want to do with Sundra next?"

"Me? You're the idea guy. Why do you think I'm buying lunch?"

"You feed me salted meat and expect my A stuff?

There better be a promise of pie attached to your next request."

"I wish I could get up off of this, but I can't. It's waking me in the middle of the night. No matter what I'm doing, I start drifting away thinking about it. I mean, Christ, I didn't even know her. Not really. I guess it's become personal because of my cousin."

Vail took the last bite of his sandwich and pushed the plate away. "You know she was a good person. If we don't give them a little extra, who do we do it for?" Vail took a drink. "I'd never say dump it. Nobody else is looking for her, so you have to. It's part of the idiot agent's code. Running in the wrong direction is our life. When we're done here, let's go back to the office and go through the file again."

"That's your great insight? Go through the file again? I could have done that."

"You're mixing up cause and effect. The insight comes when I find something in the file. If that isn't good enough, next time ask a psychic to lunch."

"Okay, okay. You ready to go?"

"What's the magic word?"

Bursaw signaled the waitress over to their booth. "Pie, please."

FIFTEEN

SITTING IN THE BACKSEAT, KATE LISTENED TO KALIX AND
Langston. Their conversation had a controlled
excitement to it. The car was positioned a good
half mile from the entrance to the park where it
was believed that James Dellasanti was going to
pick up the package left by Calculus. He thought it
was going to contain only money, while the agents
hoped for money and documents. The surveillance
crew that had gotten there first thing in the morning had found a package wrapped in black plastic
and sealed with tape. It had been found where Vail
had predicted it would be, under the end of a small
footbridge, a five-minute walk from the parking lot.

The staccato radio transmissions between the
surveillance teams at the drop site and those following Dellasanti's car cut back and forth through the
air rhythmically like a slow, efficient tennis match.
Both Langston and Kalix shifted in their seats anxiously. Kate should have been more excited about
what was getting ready to happen, but Vail's not
being there was dulling this once-in-a-career experience for her. She thought about the Russians trying
to kill him the night before and how if she had been
there he might not have been at as great a risk. After

he called her from the Oakton station, she felt sick, not because of what he'd gone through but because she hadn't taken a stronger stand against Langston's excluding him. She drew in a sobering breath and tried to not think about Vail.

She leaned her head back and started drifting off between transmissions. Every third one or so, Langston had Kalix send some unnecessary instruction. She could picture the men at the other end rolling their eyes.

"We're approaching the park," the team leader following Dellasanti said.

Langston sat up a little straighter and took the mike out of Kalix's hand. "Make sure you give him enough room. We've got people inside the park. We'll have nothing if you spook him off the pickup."

The assistant director waited a few seconds for his transmission to be rogered. The radio remained silent. Kate smiled. She knew that it was a tacit protest. This is what these agents did all day, week in and week out. The disdain that street agents developed for upper management certainly couldn't be called a mystery. "Did you copy?" Langston asked, his tone becoming more imperious. Again there was no answer, and just as Langston was about to retransmit his demand, two slow, static-punctuated pushes came from the surveillance leader's mike button, confirming that the instruction had been received.

Less than a minute later, Kate watched Dellasanti's car pass by, recognizing it from the surveillance description. Neither Langston nor Kalix seemed to notice. *"We're pulling into the parking lot,"* the team leader said.

"Let's go, John," Langston said. Kalix eased the car into gear and drove at a controlled pace through the entrance to the park. The terrain surrounding the parking lot was slightly rolling and heavily treed with hardwoods that now stood stark in the winter sunlight. In the distance ahead, winding footpaths disappeared into long stretches of evergreens. A large sign gave the park hours and listed the different trails, all coded by color.

There was about a half hour of daylight left, and a few hundred feet away, Kate could see their target exiting his car. She said, "That's him getting out of the green station wagon just ahead, John."

There were a handful of commuter cars scattered throughout the lot, and Kalix pulled into the first space he saw, turning off the engine. They watched as Dellasanti looked back once and then took off at a pace that indicated he knew where he was going, entering the trail marked "Green." The leader of the unit that had followed him handed off the "eye" to the surveillance people hidden in the park. *"Okay, Twenty-seven Three, he's all yours. We'll set up outside the entrance in case you need us to get back on him."*

"We'll keep you posted, Twelve Two."

"Come on," Langston said, opening the car door. "Did you see the way he was looking around? You could convict him on body language alone."

"A suggestion, Bill," Kate said. "I'd let the surveillance people handle this. Nobody is around. If he sees us, especially the way we're dressed, he'll make us in a heartbeat."

Langston looked down at his suit and then at Kalix. "You're probably right. We'll wait here."

The three of them listened in silence as the agents hidden in the woods described every move Dellasanti made. *"Subject has crossed the bridge and then stopped. He's looking around . . . coming around the end of the bridge . . . squatting down . . . reaching under. . . . All units, be advised the subject has the package. He's put it inside his coat and is starting back across the bridge."*

Langston held up the mike to his mouth. "All units, this is Assistant Director Langston. We'll take him when he gets to the parking lot."

"Ten-four."

Langston opened the door and grabbed a hand-held radio. "Let's go." Kalix and Kate got out. Langston and Kalix started walking quickly toward the path that Dellasanti had used to enter the park. More agents were pulling into the lot, getting out of their cars, and feeling the excitement of catching a spy red-handed; they hurried to intercept him. Kate leaned back against the car and let her mind drift off, wondering what Vail would do if he were there.

"THE GIRL ISN'T going with them!" The two men sat up straight in the same black SUV a hundred yards outside the parking lot, watching the activity through a small spotting scope.

"Patience," the passenger said, and took the scope. "As the Americans say, 'There are numerous ways to skin a cat.'" He flipped a toggle switch on the radio-transmission box sitting on the seat next to him, and a small red light lit up, indicating that it was armed.

• • •

AS SOON AS Dellasanti stepped into the clearing, Langston barked into his portable radio, "Take him!"

THE LARGE MAN sitting in the passenger seat watched carefully through the scope as the agents started to rush at Dellasanti. Calmly he pressed the button.

KATE WAS STILL leaning on the car when the package under James Dellasanti's coat exploded, cartwheeling his body through the air. All the agents charging at him dove to the ground as if expecting more detonations.

Kate ran to Dellasanti with her gun drawn, searching the perimeter for any further attack. She reached him first. He was facedown and motionless. She holstered her weapon and carefully rolled him over. A huge hole had been ripped through his overcoat. The blast had gone in the opposite direction as well. The left side of Dellasanti's rib cage was gone, and Kate could see into his body cavity. There were bits of currency around the periphery of the wound, plus some kind of cloth that had been in the package. She checked his carotid artery for a pulse and then pushed up his eyelid. He was dead.

Suddenly realizing the extent of the brutal execution she had just witnessed, Kate collapsed into a sitting position on the ground. Her adrenaline subsided as quickly as it had risen, and her mind fell into a stupor. It took all her strength not to vomit.

ALTHOUGH VAIL WAS at the off-site reading some of the missing-analyst reports that Bursaw had discreetly copied for him, his mind kept straying to the Calculus case. He tried to shrug the thoughts off, but still something in his subconscious was sending up a small flare of protest. He stepped over to the wall covered with the details of the case and started tracing the intricate web of clues that the Russian had left.

The phone rang. It was Bursaw. "Denise just called. Our guy came back."

"Is he there now?"

"Have we ever been that lucky?"

"Your voice sounds like there's good news in there somewhere."

"She got his plate."

"I hope you're calling from your car."

"I'll be there in fifteen minutes."

WHEN VAIL GOT into Bursaw's Bureau car, he took a moment to read his friend's face. There were tiny creases of excitement at the corners of his eyes. "I guess you think this is your guy."

He pulled away from the curb. "My guy, I don't know. But the guy who killed these prostitutes, yeah, I think this is him. As far as him being responsible for Sundra, it's a leap from hookers to middle-class

FBI analysts, even if they are all black. But I've got nothing else going right now." He looked over at Vail. "Besides, this is like a time machine, you and me on the street, at night, freezing cold, trying to find some animal that has a million places to hide."

"I think you're remembering only the good parts."

Bursaw laughed in disbelief. "Tell me you don't miss it."

"Not enough to reenlist."

"So you'd rather be a bricklayer?"

"You sound like Kate. She thinks I should do something more meaningful, but I have no complaints. I've tried to figure out why. The way my old man shoved it down my throat when I was a kid, hating it would make more sense."

"'Having no complaints' is a long way from being passionate about something," Bursaw said.

As Bursaw slowed the car and started looking for the address from the plate Denise Washington had supplied, Vail said, "There's our van," pointing to the vehicle the prostitute had described.

Bursaw drove a block farther and turned around. "That's a nasty-looking apartment building it's parked in front of."

"Are we going in?" Vail asked.

"We'd have to get real lucky to find him in there. The apartments won't be marked and the bells never work. And no one in there is going to help the *po*-lice." Bursaw checked his watch. "It's after midnight, too late for him to go cruising. And I'm not going to sit on it all night." He put the car in park, got out, and went to the trunk. Vail watched as he walked toward the van, a pair of pliers in one hand and a wire in the other. He started stripping the ends.

When he reached the van, Bursaw looked around casually before lifting the engine cover. In less than a minute, the van's horn started blaring. He lowered the hood and walked back to the car. "Let's just hope his apartment is close enough to the street for him to hear that."

The two men watched the windows at the front of the apartment building as a couple of lights came on. Five minutes later a black man in his early thirties with a shaved head came out and unlocked the van's door. They could see him pushing angrily on the horn, trying to get it to release.

Bursaw put the Bureau car in gear. "Get a big mouthful of this warm air, because if this moron runs, he's all yours, Steve."

They pulled up to the van, and Vail rolled down his window. "Can we give you a hand, sir?"

The man turned and started to say something. But then he saw that the two men were law enforcement. "No, that's all right, I got it." He disappeared around the front of his van and raised the hood.

As quietly as possible, Vail opened the car door. Bursaw said, "Hey, Steve, remember that time in Detroit when you left me outside to cover the back of that house for an hour in below-zero weather? Remember how sick I got?"

Vail looked back inside the car and saw Bursaw's hand move to the siren switch with the impending ceremony of a symphony conductor. Vail started to laugh. "Come on, Luke, don't. I'm begging you."

"I know what a proponent of revenge you are, so this is for you." Bursaw flicked the switch on and off rapidly. It gave a brief yelp. Vail hurried around the front of the van. The man turned quickly and slashed at Vail's face with a screwdriver. Vail fell back out of the way, and it was all the delay the man needed to take off running.

Vail looked at Bursaw, who was laughing. "Keep laughing and I'll let this guy get away."

"It's impossible for you to let anyone get away with anything," Bursaw said. "The idiot agent's code, remember?"

Vail took off at a dead run. Bursaw pulled the car up next to him and drove at the same speed. "A white man chasing a black man. Sounds like we're about to have a violation of civil rights."

Vail glanced over at him and tried to look angry.

"Appears like you've lost a step since Detroit. Get those knees up, Vail. I think you're losing him. Knees up."

Vail struggled not to laugh. It was hard enough running in the cold air. He watched as Bursaw pulled ahead and turned right.

Vail could still see the man almost a block ahead of him now, also turning right. Somehow Bursaw had guessed correctly. Vail pushed himself harder. When he got to the corner and turned, the man was gone. And there was no place to hide. Vail sprinted to the next corner and looked both ways. To the left, half a block up, Bursaw had the man pinned against the car and was applying some sort of jujitsu arm bar, causing the man to rise to his tiptoes and whimper in pain.

Vail ran up and handcuffed him. Bursaw pulled out the man's wallet. "Mr. Jonathan Wilkins. Congratulations, you have just received a demonstration of the old hammer-and-anvil tactic, which goes all the way back to Alexander the Great." When Wilkins didn't say anything, Bursaw said, "Not a history buff, huh, Jonathan?"

"I didn't do nothing," Wilkins said.

"You know, Jonathan, I'm really starting to hate my job. In the fifteen years I've been with the FBI, not once have I arrested the right man." Bursaw pushed him into the backseat, and Vail got in next to him. As they drove to the Washington Field Office, Vail advised him of his rights.

VAIL WATCHED THE monitor as Bursaw started interviewing Wilkins. There was no table or desk between them, and the black agent was in the prisoner's body space, their knees almost touching. Bursaw handed Wilkins the photographs of the three dead prostitutes. "Ever see these girls?"

Wilkins looked at the photos, trying to appear disinterested. "No."

"They're prostitutes. Ever go out with a prostitute?"

"Never paid for it in my life."

Bursaw noted his overall slovenliness. "A real ladies' man, huh, Jonathan?"

"I do all right."

Bursaw held up the photos fanned out. "You're sure you don't know any of these women." Wilkins kept his eyes down, refusing to look at the photos again. "Jonathan, look at me." Without looking at the photos, Wilkins's eyes found Bursaw's. "This is very important. You've never seen any of these women before?"

"No."

"Then I'm assuming it would not be possible for your semen to be found inside them."

Vail could see the statement hit home. Wilkins's posture pulled back defensively. It was unusual for a psychopathic killer to have such poor lying skills, but his reaction left little doubt that he had killed the three women.

"Unless somebody planted it there."

Bursaw smiled crookedly. "Are you in the habit of giving your sperm to people who would want to frame you?"

"You said they're prostitutes. Maybe I, you know, had a date with them or something."

"So you have paid for it."

"Sometimes. You know a man's got to be a man. Don't like to admit it, though."

"I understand, Jonathan." Bursaw leaned closer and lowered his voice. "Since we're both telling the truth here, I'm going to tell you something you've got to promise not to tell anyone."

"What?"

Bursaw leaned in another inch. "I don't care about these three whores. I only care about this woman." He showed Wilkins a photo of Sundra Boston.

This time Wilkins studied the photo before answering. "Man, *her* I don't know."

Bursaw looked up at the hidden camera and gave an almost imperceptible shake of his head, letting Vail know that it was apparent that Wilkins had nothing to do with Sundra Boston's disappearance. "Take off your shirt, man."

"I don't have to," Wilkins said.

"Did you want another jujitsu lesson?" Reluctantly, Wilkins pulled his shirt over his head while he glared at Bursaw. There was a three-inch scar on his chest that looked like it could have been caused by the screwdriver attack Denise Washington had described. "See, Jonathan, that scar was caused by a screwdriver, and we have the witness who did it to you. She'll testify about you trying to tie her up in the van, like the other three were. And we'll find their DNA in your van and on those ropes, which I'm sure you didn't bother to change each time. I'm sorry, man, it's over." Bursaw let it all sink in for a few seconds and then said, "But like I told you, I don't care about those three, just this one." Again he held up Sundra's photo. "Tell you what I'll do. We have her killer's DNA, so if you'll give me a sample of yours to prove that you weren't involved in her death, you and I will be done."

"I'll give you DNA, hair, blood whatever you want," Wilkins said, pointing at Sundra's photo. "But you can't use it for the others."

"Agreed." Bursaw opened his briefcase and took out a cheek-swab kit, extracting a long Q-tip. "Open up."

Wilkins opened his mouth, and Bursaw got the swab to within an inch of Wilkins's cheek before breaking it in half and throwing it on the table. "You've convinced me, Jonathan. You had nothing to do with Sundra's disappearance."

"Then I can go?"

"Not just yet." Bursaw stood him up and hand-cuffed him. "I think the Metro police are going to want to talk to you."

IT WAS A little after 4 A.M. when Vail and Bursaw dropped Wilkins at the Washington Metropolitan Police homicide unit. Forty-five minutes later, Luke Bursaw pulled up in front of the off-site. "Any idea what you're going to do now?" Vail asked.

"Sleep and not think about it for a while. Do you have any idea how much longer you're going to be around?"

"I think this other thing is getting close to being resolved." Vail handed him a key. "In case something comes up, take this. The alarm code is 9111."

"Does that mean it's going well or it's going badly?"

"We're making progress. Unfortunately, it's in the form of one disaster after another."

"Just remember, when it comes to the government, disasters aren't necessarily bad. If nothing else, it means somebody is doing something."

Vail got out and started toward the door when Bursaw hit the siren with another brief yelp.

VAIL HAD STARTED to undress when the phone rang. It was almost six in the morning. Chances that this call was good news were not high.

It was Kate. "Dellasanti's dead."

"How?"

"There was a bomb in the package. As we were closing in on him, it exploded."

"Did he set it off?"

"We don't know. It didn't go off until he saw us coming. So either he committed suicide to keep from going to prison or Calculus put it in the package. Which doesn't make any sense."

"Or maybe the Russians did it to make sure the thread between the pieces of evidence would be broken once and for all. Then we couldn't go any further."

Kate said, "I hadn't thought of that. It's definitely a possibility, the way they've been killing their sources."

"Where are you now?"

"I'm still at the park. Langston's got three forensics teams here processing the scene, and we're just about done. He's ordered all the autopsy and lab work be done by noon so we can get a couple of hours' sleep. There's a meeting in his office, at noon, to analyze everything. He wants you there."

"Okay."

"Really? I thought you'd take the opportunity to ride off into the sunset, yelling 'I told you so' over your shoulder."

"Dellasanti would be just as dead if I had been there. Did any of the evidence survive?"

"I don't think any of the money did. We're not sure about the documents. Something was blown into Dellasanti's body cavity. We decided to let the medical examiner extract it."

"Are you doing all right?"

"I'm seeing a few more bodies than I'd like, but I'm fine."

"I'll see you at noon."

SIXTEEN

THE THREE UNIT AND SECTION CHIEFS WERE ALREADY SEATED in the director's conference room when Vail walked in. Kate was getting coffee from a side table. Vail went over and poured himself a cup.

"You look like you didn't get much sleep," she said.

"I was out celebrating not killing Dellasanti."

"With any luck there are a couple spies left so you can get your batting average back up."

Langston hurried into the room followed by John Kalix, who was carrying a stack of files. "We're in the director's conference room because he wanted to attend this meeting, but at the last moment he was called before a congressional oversight committee."

Vail leaned close to Kate. "Hopefully that isn't about us."

"The good thing is, you'll probably be fired and back in Chicago by the time Congress gets the final body count."

"You really are a silver-lining kind of girl, aren't you?"

Langston sat down at the head of the table. "As if our latest spy getting killed wasn't bad enough, the lab was unable to find anything to give us a clue as to the identity of the next one."

The section chief, Tony Battly, said, "Maybe there are no more. Calculus said the last one would be an intelligence agent. I suppose someone in the State Department could be considered in intelligence."

Somebody said, "Apparently you haven't spent much time around the State Department."

"Or maybe he instructed his relative at the Chicago bank to get us the name after the payments for the first three are deposited," Mark Brogdon said. "Bill, you've had me pay the first two—should I wire another quarter of a million for this one and see what happens?"

Langston said, "We've already sent them half a million dollars. That seems like we'd be throwing more money away."

"I know, but on the off chance that the relative can help us, I think we should consider it. The money's already been earmarked for this."

Vail said, "If you send them a quarter of a million and Dellasanti was the intelligence agent, maybe they would somehow let us know we owe them another quarter of a million. Then we'd be sure he was the big fish and be through with this."

Langston said, "You're right. Besides, it's not like the money's coming out of my pocket. Make the payment, Mark." Nervously, the assistant director straightened his tie. "Anything else, Steve?"

"Mind if *I* see the reports?"

"Sure, you may." Langston pushed them down to him. "What exactly are you looking for?"

"Kate, tell them," he said as he started scanning the reports.

"Anomalies," she answered in an amused tone.

As Vail continued to read, flipping past boiler-plate pages, everyone sat quietly and wondered if he would find something that they'd all missed. The lab had recovered a small piece of a circuit used in remote-control devices. That meant that Dellasanti had not killed himself, and neither had Calculus. It had to be the Russians waiting until the last possible second before disposing of a potentially embarrassing double agent, something they had now done twice before. "I'm not going to find anything in the lab reports," Vail said. "Those guys are too thorough. Was there anything left from the package?"

Kate thought Vail's tone was a little too civil. He had to be hiding something.

"The one with the dark blue cover has photographs of everything," Kalix said.

Vail started through the pictures. "What's this one?" He held it up to Kalix.

"It's some sort of sleeve. A packet of money was inside it and intact. The lab is doing more testing on it. It's some kind of material that is virtually indestructible. The best guess is that it might be from the days of the diplomatic pouch, to protect documents."

"Our diplomats or theirs?"

"At this point we have no idea."

Vail went back to the photos. "Let me have a couple of minutes."

A clerk came in with a tray of fresh coffee. The others got up and poured themselves a cup. Kate brought one to Vail and set it next to him. Focused on the photographs, he didn't seem to notice. The men stood around saying little, occasionally glancing over at Vail, trying to see which photographs he was looking at.

Inside the protective sleeve had been two bundles of banded fifty-dollar bills. Finally Vail closed the file. Without a word, everyone sat down. "Bill, can I see the money?"

Langston nodded to Kalix, who went to the nearest phone. "Did you find something?"

"Not really. That's why I'd like to see the actual items." He picked up his coffee and took a swallow. "Thanks, Kate."

Ten minutes later a woman in a gray lab smock walked in with a cardboard box, and Langston told her to give it to Vail. Each bundle of fifties was in a clear plastic envelope. They all had the same purple tinge to them after being fumed for fingerprints. Vail lifted each stack out carefully, examining both sides before setting it down. Finally he picked up one of the bundles and riffled through it. He opened the file and checked the photos of the bills, trying to make out the serial numbers. "Here's a question I hope someone can answer: Are these bills in their original order? You know, before they were fumed." He looked from face to face, but no one replied. "That's what I was afraid of."

Finally Kalix said, "Wait. There were lists made of the bills." He picked up another folder and flipped through it. "Yes, here they are. I assume they're listed in order."

Vail examined the list. "Very good. If you're right."

"What is it, Vail?" Langston asked.

He was still examining the money. "The bills are nonsequential, which is the way spies are supposed to be paid. Did anyone consider the way they're arranged in the stacks? Like taking the first digit from the top ten bills? If this is what Calculus intended, I don't know which stack would be the coded stack. Maybe it's the last ten bills in one of the stacks. Get ahold of whoever made the list and ask him if any of the bills were upside down or backward. If that is the code Calculus used, it's going to take more work to untangle, which isn't surprising, since his clues seem to get more complicated as they go along. That's the only thing I can see. But if there was a clue, maybe it was on the documents." He looked around the table and was surprised that no one seemed to realize that the Russians had put the package together and that as a result there would be no clues. But Vail wanted them to be kept busy. He had seen something in the photographs.

Langston said to Kalix, "Get somebody up here from Cryptanalysis." Then he turned to the group. "We're starting to get calls from the media regarding the bombing at the park yesterday. Once again, refer them to Public Affairs. It's only a matter of time until they start putting together the other deaths with this one. Let's hope we'll be done by then and we can let them know what we've accomplished. If no one has anything else, that's it."

Kate said to Vail, "Speaking of the media, I

heard an interesting item on the radio this morning. Seems two FBI agents caught a serial murderer last night and dropped him off at the locals. Know anything about that?"

He smiled. "I don't know, I don't have a radio."

"It *was* you."

"Actually, it was Luke. But unfortunately it had nothing to do with his missing analyst."

"And where are you off to now?"

"I don't know. I'll find something to do. There are a lot of computer records I need to look through for Luke."

"That's twice in the last ten seconds you've said 'I don't know,' which isn't a commonly used Steve Vail line. You've figured out something, haven't you?"

"You think I'm keeping something from Luke?"

Kate lowered her voice to a whisper. "I'm talking about this." She pointed to the material on the table.

"I just gave you and the rest of the brain trust the only lead I could think of. As a tactic, your accusing me of not being forthcoming is getting a little old."

"That's because it's usually true."

"Listen, I've given you people everything in this case, and what did I get for my trouble? I got cut out."

" '*You people*'? Cutting you out wasn't my doing."

"I didn't hear you objecting. I know we're not happening, but you were supposed to protect our interests and get me first crack at the evidence. So when do I see it? When the guys who the director supposedly can't trust with the investigation are done pawing over it. Do you think if they do find anything in those bills, I'm going to get a call? It's a different year, but these are the same people who ran me out of the Bureau five years ago. They'll always be the people who cripple this organization." Vail stared at her as if making some judgment. "You want to know where I'm going—I'm going to pack."

Kate wanted to say something, but she knew he was right, not only about who ran the FBI but also about her not standing up for him. Vail was the reason they'd accomplished what they had. He was the one who had survived two attempts to kill him. Against his wishes, he had agreed to work on the case. And in return he only wanted to conduct the investigation his own way. Which was exactly why he had been brought in. Until completed, he believed the challenge belonged only to him.

Suddenly she was overwhelmed with the perverse hope that with Vail gone they wouldn't find the last spy, if there was one. Without Vail they might never identify him. She wanted them to fail, all of them, herself included.

VAIL TOLD HIMSELF to slow down as he drove back to the off-site. He had not been as upset with Kate as he had pretended. Although he was disappointed that he wasn't allowed to be involved in Dellasanti's arrest or get first look at what had been recovered, he knew that inevitably men like Langston couldn't live with someone else being perceived as the point man. Vail had warned everyone that it would happen, even though they assured him that this time it wouldn't.

He knew that what had happened to Dellasanti wasn't Langston's fault, but right now the investigation had been brought to a halt. Vail had no choice but to proceed by himself. He'd given Langston and the others the serial-number possibility because he knew that the combinations would be infinite and would keep them busy while he checked out what he'd seen in the photos.

He parked outside the off-site and went upstairs. He needed to recheck Calculus's movements the day he'd originally planted Dellasanti's package in the park. After putting it under the bridge, he had walked around the area for a couple of minutes, not something spies do. The longer you're there, the greater your chances of being connected to whatever you left behind. Get in fast, get out faster.

He turned on the computer and went to the wall with a pencil and paper. All the coordinates and times at the park varied little as Calculus moved around those few minutes after being at the bridge. Then Vail went back to the computer and linked onto the Bureau satellite. After zooming down into the park, he carefully manipulated the mouse until he could see Calculus's exact path that day. Did it indicate that he'd hidden something else? Something, even under torture, he hadn't told the Russians about? It would be a way for a dying man to get even with them. Retracing the movements once more on the computer, Vail memorized the terrain Calculus had moved through.

It was a little over an hour's drive to the park in Maryland in the early-afternoon traffic. He parked in the same lot where James Dellasanti had been killed the day before. At the entrance to a footpath, he saw small traces of blood where the body had lain on the ground. He looked around and decided there were a number of different locations from which the bomb could have been detonated.

The footbridge where the package of evidence had been secreted was about a quarter of a mile in, about a five-minute walk along the winding path. Included in the pictures he had seen that morning was a shot of the exact spot where the plastic-wrapped material had been picked up. It was an all-metal bridge, cleverly constructed almost entirely of two-inch-square steel tubes. About twenty feet long, it sat less than two feet above a small brook, which was dry this time of year.

He stepped down into the streambed and tried to re-create the angle at which the photographer had taken the picture. What had caught his attention was a small mark on one of the five steel tubes that ran under the bridge's flooring pieces as supports. At least he thought it was a mark. It was hard to tell in the photograph; it looked like an elongated checkmark or a single-barb arrow, pointing down. He had seen similar ink markings in engineering drawings, and since Calculus was a trained engineer, it could have been made by him. With each clue left for the FBI, subtlety had become the Russian agent's signature. And the mark had been the same medium blue as Vail had encountered twice before on items left by Calculus.

There it was. He moved closer. It was an abbreviated arrow drawn in blue marker, its line thin and barely noticeable. But pointing to what? There was only about a foot between the sloping stream bank underneath it and the supporting steel tube. Reaching under it, he probed it with his fingers but couldn't feel anything. He checked the arrow again and wondered if it meant that something was buried in the streambed directly below.

The ground was mostly sand and stone, now stiffened by winter temperatures. Any attempt to dig it up would have been difficult to disguise, and to his eye the streambed appeared undisturbed. He looked more closely at the arrow. The square tubing had rounded corners, and the arrow was drawn completely on the side except for the point, which wrapped slightly underneath the tube. Vail got down on his back and shimmied under the bridge. Drawn in the same blue ink on the underside of the tube were two concentric circles inside an oval, a simple rendering of an eyeball.

Vail stood up and took off his topcoat, brushing the back of it while he thought. After a few moments, he decided he had no idea what Calculus had intended. Maybe it was one of those instances of being too close to something to accurately assess it.

Walking back fifty feet along the bank of the small stream, he examined the structure. The steel tubes supporting the walkway were completely hollow, and from that distance he could actually see light coming through the one with the arrow drawn on it.

That was it.

He hurried back to the bridge and squatted down so he could look through the marked tube. The only thing directly in his line of sight, thirty yards on the other side, was a sign marking the path in case of snowfall. Because its purpose was seasonal, it was set in a concrete-filled rubber tire that allowed it to be taken away and stored during warmer weather. Apparently Calculus had moved it so it could be sighted through the steel tube.

Walking over to the sign, Vail tipped it over. The base was hollow. He reached up under it and could feel a small plastic-wrapped object taped to the inside. He pulled it out and opened it. It was a computer flash drive, a device about the size of a thumb that was capable of storing a large amount of digital information. Its shell was plastic and on the back side, handwritten in Cyrillic, was the word *конец*. If Vail remembered his college Russian correctly, it meant "the end." Apparently this was the last spy that Calculus was going to lead them to.

конец

Vail put the device in his pocket, along with the plastic it had been wrapped in, and headed for his car.

As he came off the footpath into the parking lot, he was stunned to see Langston and Kalix standing next to their car. There were four other cars in the lot, each with a lone driver—FBI surveillance.

Vail couldn't believe that he'd been followed and hadn't noticed. He scanned the sky looking for a Bureau airplane. There didn't appear to be any, at least not any longer. After his three years as an agent in Detroit, he had always been surveillance-conscious. Even when he returned to the everyday

existence of a bricklayer, he couldn't help being vig-
ilant. But, more important, he wondered what had
made them follow him. He'd given them a plausible
distraction, which apparently they hadn't bitten on.
Had he underestimated them? Then he thought of
Kate. She was probably the only one capable of figuring out what he was up to. She had even accused
him of it after the meeting. But it was hard for him
to believe that she would have given him up.

Without a word, Vail walked over to Langston
and handed him the flash drive. "And whatever it
was wrapped in," the assistant director demanded.

Vail pulled the section of plastic out of his coat
pocket and gave it to him. "I guess I underestimated
you," Vail said. It was a statement of apparent surrender carefully designed to judge Langston's reaction, to see if following him had been his idea or
someone else's.

"One of arrogance's consequences," Langston
said, his response giving no clues.

Vail smiled and shrugged his shoulders. "Then it
would appear that my work here is done." He took
off his Glock and handed it to Kalix, along with his
credentials. "As always, working with management
has been a delight."

"The real question is not whether you underestimated us but whether you overrated yourself,"
Langston said. "Please be out of the off-site by noon
tomorrow."

Vail watched the two men get into their car and
speed out of the lot. The four surveillance vehicles
fell into line behind them and within seconds were
gone.

SEVENTEEN

ONCE VAIL REACHED THE HIGHWAY, HE STAYED IN THE RIGHT lane and drove at the posted speed limit, forcing cars to stream around him so he could lose himself in thought. He still couldn't believe that he'd missed the surveillance. But being followed wasn't the issue. He was using it to avoid thinking about the possibility that Kate had told Langston of his deception. Someone had figured out what he was doing, and the others in the room didn't seem to possess the aptitude to get a read on him that easily. Kate knew how, given the slightest opportunity, he gladly sent bosses in the wrong direction. If it had been anyone but her, he would just have confronted the person, but he realized now that he was afraid what he might find out.

As soon as he arrived at the off-site, Vail called the airline and made a reservation to Miami early the next morning. He still had his wreck-diving trip to look forward to. Not that he'd enjoy it now. But at least it would be warm and provide enough of a distraction that he wouldn't dwell on how this had ended. He made himself a sandwich and ate only half of it. Fatigue burned his eyes, and his thoughts kept wandering off into meaningless directions when he tried to avoid thinking about her. Maybe if he slept for a while, the confusion would disappear.

He lay down on the cot and forced his eyes closed. After a few minutes, he knew he wouldn't be able to sleep. He got up and, to busy himself with mindless work, started packing. He should call Luke Bursaw and let him know that he was leaving, but he had no desire to talk to anyone. Once he got back to Chicago, he would call him and apologize for the abrupt departure. He felt bad about leaving the analyst case unresolved, but Bursaw was a tenacious investigator and in time would find the answer on his own. Vail pulled on his topcoat, picked up the car keys, and headed out the door. There was a bar less than four blocks away.

IT WAS A little after 2 A.M. when Vail woke up to someone pounding on the front door. He could still taste the Irish whiskey in his mouth, reminding him why the thumping was so irritating. When he finally opened the door, he was surprised to see John Kalix standing there.

"What's the matter?" Vail asked.

"It's Kate. She's been arrested."

"What?"

"I'm sorry, Steve, it's true. That flash drive you recovered, it named the intelligence agent who Calculus promised. It was Kate."

Vail laughed without humor. "That's absurd."

"That was my first reaction, too, but the evidence is overwhelming. There was a typed list of